FLAG IN HIDING

FLAG
IN
HIDING

BY TRELLA LAMSON DICK

Illustrated by Don Bolognese

ABELARD-SCHUMAN
LONDON AND NEW YORK

FLAG IN HIDING

CHAPTER *1*

The windows of Master Bundy's schoolroom were shut against the soft June breeze. In the stuffy atmosphere a dozen children droned their spelling aloud. Master Bundy sat at his desk, ferule in hand, his eyes downcast either in thought or drowsiness. It was never safe to assume that Master Bundy dozed, so no child ceased to mumble his words.

Bang! The heavy stroke of the ferule on the desk made everyone jump. "Speech time," said the schoolmaster. At once shoulders straightened and smiles replaced listless looks. Speech time was a welcome change from studying spelling or doing sums.

"Speech time!" Master Bundy repeated, standing straight and tall before them in his broadcloth and white ruffles. His hair, brown and unpowdered, was gathered neatly into a queue and enclosed in a black silk sack. A proper-looking man, indeed, was the schoolmaster.

His voice was pleasant as he asked, "Who has a speech today? Randy Stewart, how about you? It is long since you have favored us with aught save the first five verses of Genesis."

A titter swept the room. Cynthia, Randy's

7

twelve-year-old sister, looked about angrily. Laugh at Randy, would they, because he didn't like to learn speeches! Why, he was the cleverest in the room at sums or history. Master Bundy himself said so.

Her anger turned to amazement as she saw Randy rise and come forward. His voice was eager, not drawly as usual, as he said, "Yes sir, I have a speech—a grand speech."

When had he learned it, Cynthia wondered. She eyed her brother fearfully. Surely he wouldn't tease Master Bundy with those five verses from Genesis again! If he did, he'd get a tanning sure.

Master Bundy, too, was eying Randy in surprise. "If it's 'In the beginning—'"

"It isn't, sir, but it's words as wonderful."

"Let's hear this masterpiece," the schoolmaster said. "It had better be good." He fingered his ferule suggestively.

"It is good." Randy's tone was so confident it impressed his listeners. There was a hush as he stepped forward.

He was tall for his fourteen years, and stood erect. His head was thrown back, his eyes gazing far away at something wonderful. It made Cynthia's breath come quick to see him. But what could he be going to say?

His voice, not loud, rang like a bell through the room. "Is life so dear, or peace so sweet, as to be

purchased at the price of chains and slavery? Forbid it, Almighty God!"

"Randy!" Master Bundy's voice was harsh with urgency. "Randy, stop—stop—"

There was no stopping Randy. "I care not what course others may take, but as for me, give me liberty or give me death."

Randy faced the schoolmaster. "Are they not great words? Can you find greater in the Bible?"

Master Bundy's face was white, his voice thick, as he said, "Blasphemy! Blasphemous and traitorous utterance! Is there no shame in you? Come here!"

Randy still held his head high. "You can beat me, but won't you agree they are wonderful words? Won't you?"

"Come here!"

Never had Cynthia heard the schoolmaster speak in such a terrible tone. It frightened her as much as the sound of the ferule on Randy's back. She buried her face in her hands to shut out sight and sound.

"I hated him," she told Randy as they went home that afternoon. "Mostly I like Master Bundy, but not when he beats you. I wanted to fly at him and scratch his eyes out. But I am a coward. All I could do was sit and cry."

"You couldn't have helped." Randy walked down the woods path, his shoulders bowed.

Cynthia, stepping along behind him, looked at

10

her brother pityingly. Usually when Randy got out of school he was like their sorrel colt, prancing and kicking up his heels. Today he plodded along like old Maje, the work horse.

"Did he hurt you pretty badly?" she asked.

Randy turned to her, his face grim. "Yes, he hurt me, but not with the ferule. He hurt me when he showed himself a coward.

"What do you mean?"

"When he wouldn't admit they were great words. When he was afraid to have me say them." He was thoughtful for a moment, then added, "You know, Sis, I had a feeling that they made him feel as they did me. For a moment I saw it in his eyes."

"You might have known it would make Master Bundy angry. It *did* sound traitorous. Why can't you say something proper, like the twenty-third psalm?"

"Proper! Oh, what's the use of talking to a featherbrain who doesn't care about anything but pretty clothes!"

"Why Randy Stewart, what a way to talk to your sister!" But Cynthia was too curious to stay angry. "Wherever did you learn that, Randy? It was strange and not easy to forget."

"*Don't* forget it, Cynthia. That's what the man said to me. 'Don't forget it, boy. Let it ring in your mind like a bell—liberty or death, one or the other—men have to choose!'"

11

"What man told you, Randy?"

A smile broke the seriousness of Randy's face. "A voice crying in the wilderness told me."

"Now you're teasing me and I don't think it's a bit nice." Cynthia tossed her head angrily. Presently she heard him muttering something. Then the words came more loudly through the quiet woods, "I care not what course others may take—"

Randy broke off suddenly and grabbed up a stone. "There's a varmint behind that boulder, Sis. Watch me knock his head off."

A tousled head popped up from behind the rock. "Don't throw it," squeaked a terrified voice. A boy about Cynthia's age, in ragged, dirty clothes, stood up, his bright gaze like that of a cornered animal.

"If it isn't peeping Peter!" Randy's tone was contemptuous. He dropped the stone. "Some day that spying habit's going to cost you a split head." He turned and resumed his march.

Peter Estry leaned on the boulder, the fear gone from his black eyes, only spite remaining. "You seem to like the words better than the schoolmaster does," he taunted.

Randy walked on, not bothering to reply.

"Going to tell your father you got a tanning?"

"That's none of your affair," Cynthia said, hurrying after Randy. When they were well out of Peter's hearing, she said, "Randy, don't tell Father about the whipping you got. I won't, and then—"

12

"You heard Master Bundy order me to tell Father. You heard me promise I would."

"Yes, but—"

"Enough said. I keep my promises."

"But Randy—" Cynthia's voice trembled—"Father whips even harder than Master Bundy."

"How well I know it!"

"It makes Mother feel so bad when you get whipped. Don't you think for her sake—"

"No." Randy turned toward his sister. "Master Bundy told me to say those words to Father and I'm going to. They won't seem traitorous and like blasphemy to him, I warrant." He gave Cynthia a sidewise glance. "I wonder if you really know about Father?"

Cynthia tossed her head. "Of course I do. You and Father, and Mother too, treat me as if I were Polly's age. I know what's going on. I understand."

"Well, then, see that you keep still," Randy ordered sternly. "Don't be telling things to Dencie."

"You're a fine one to scold about not telling things," Cynthia answered. "You know you shouldn't have made that speech today. When the squire hears about it, it may make trouble for Father."

Randy sighed heavily. "I know it was wrong. But the words kept saying themselves in my mind until I had to say them out loud. I wanted to see what they would do to Master Bundy. All they

13

did was make him rarin' mad. He never beat me that hard before."

He walked on in silence for a little, then said, "Father'll be angry and with good right. I promised him I'd be careful. He'll feel he can't trust me, and I guess he can't. I get carried away. I want to shout out to those Tories what I really think."

"Hush, Randy, please hush." Cynthia began singing a doleful hymn at the top of her voice to drown out further dangerous remarks.

Soon they came to the edge of the woods. Before them lay the fields and buildings of home, snug and comfortable in the afternoon sun. A sturdy log house stood in the middle of the clearing with other buildings clustered near. Beyond on every side were fields and meadows. In one field they could see their father working. Chickens, geese and ducks were busy in the barnyard. From a distant field came the worried bleating of lambs and the hoarse answering voices of the ewes.

"Doesn't it look peaceful and happy!" Cynthia exclaimed.

"Yes," Randy agreed. "It's worth fighting for."

"You mean fighting the Indians?" Cynthia asked.

"No, I don't mean Indians."

Tip, the shepherd dog, came bounding over the field and followed them down the lane.

14

The house yard was enclosed in a split log fence to keep the fowls out. In the shade of a tree, Polly, their four-year-old sister, was playing. She was rocking the cat in the doll cradle, singing softly words about fairies. Randy and Cynthia smiled at each other as they listened.

Tip gave a bark of disgust at the sight of Primrose the cat getting so much attention. Polly looked up. "Sssh!" She held up a warning finger. "Primmie's asleep. Don't wake her." She tiptoed to Randy. "Ride me," she ordered.

Randy lifted her to his shoulders and marched to the house. "We're home," he shouted as they stepped on the porch. "Mother, we're—"

"So am I. Stop your shouting." Their mother emerged from the shadowy recesses of the buttery carrying a crock of milk.

How pretty Mother was, thought Cynthia. Her curly brown hair kept escaping in soft tendrils from the net. Her complexion was creamy. She had merry brown eyes and a dimple which played hide-and-seek near the corner of her mouth.

"Learn anything today?" she asked as they en-

15

tered the kitchen. It was her usual question and they expected it. Today Randy hesitated so long that Cynthia looked at him anxiously.

"Yes," he said at last. "I learned something."

"Master Bundy told us about Alexander the Great," Cynthia said quickly. "It was interesting, wasn't it, Randy?"

Randy set Polly down. "It was interesting if you cared what happened long ago. I—"

"What's for supper, Mother?" Cynthia interrupted. "Randy and I are starved. I hope there's dried apple pie."

"Goodness, child, how you rattle on!" her mother exclaimed. "Get your dress changed and set the table. Randy, we'll hear what you learned after supper. Your father would like to hear it, too."

"I want him to hear it," Randy said. "I'll fill the woodbin now."

Cynthia was glad Randy would wait until after supper to tell his unpleasant news. She hoped he wouldn't say anything disrespectful about Master Bundy. That would make Father angry. He had a high regard for teachers. She was sure, though, that Randy couldn't escape a beating. "Get a whipping at school and you get one at home," was Father's rule.

She climbed the stairs to the shadowy loft. It was divided into two rooms which were high enough to stand erect in only at the middle because of the sharply slanting roof. Randy's room was the one where the stairs came up. She and Polly shared the other. The furnishings were simple. The bed was handhewn with woven ropes to hold the mattress and straw tick. There were linen sheets woven by her mother, and a blanket of fine wool. Cynthia herself had made the gay, quilted bedspread with its hundreds of tiny squares of bright calico.

Her father had made the walnut commode which held wash-bowl and pitcher. A carpet of rags was on the floor. Two samplers which Cynthia had made adorned the walls. A settee completed the furnishings.

Cynthia looked around the room with pride as she carefully took off her white ruffled pinafore and hung it on a peg. No girl she knew had such a nice room except Dencie, Squire Telford's daughter. The Squire's fine stone mansion was furnished with elegant things from England.

"But I'd rather have my room and my father than Dencie's room and that cranky old father of hers." Cynthia gave a shrug of distaste. Then catching sight of herself in the mirror she changed her expression hastily. If she was going to be as pretty as her mother, she must practice looking sweet. When she smiled just right, she had a dimple, too. She practiced smiling until her mother called,

"Cynthia—hurry, child." Then she quickly took off her merino dress, put on an old linsey-woolsey, and went down the ladder.

Dusk had begun to fill the kitchen. She lit candles for the mantel and table. By the time supper was dished up, Randy had the woodbox filled and Father came in. After he had washed himself and combed his hair into a neat queue, he led the way to the table. The short grace was said standing.

Father sat at the head of the table in a stout chair of his own making. Mother was at the other end with Polly beside her. Cynthia and Randy sat together on a bench. The table was made of walnut, heavy and strong. The linen cloth was hand-woven with napkins to match. Pewter spoons, knives and plates were used. Silver and china were reserved for company use.

There was a large bowl of stew made from venison and vegetables. There was hot buttered cornbread, and homemade cheese. Dessert was hasty pudding with maple syrup.

After supper Cynthia brought her father his pipe and tobacco. With the pipe tongs, she carried a coal from the hearth to light it. Mr. Stewart sat back comfortably in his chair while Mother and Cynthia cleared the table. Polly lay on a rug before the fire with Primrose on one side and Tip on the other.

"Daydreaming, son?" Mr. Stewart asked Randy,

who was still sitting on the bench. "Remember you have chores to do."

Cynthia drew a tremulous breath and thought, Here it comes! Please, Father, don't whip him. Be careful, Randy; don't make Father angry.

Her mixed-up thoughts were interrupted by Randy's sober question, "Father, why did Grandpa Stewart leave New York City and come way up here on the Hudson to a wild country?"

Mr. Stewart took his pipe from his mouth and looked at his son. "Seems to me I've told you that before."

"Why did he? Please tell me again, Father."

Mr. Stewart leaned forward, shaking his pipe for emphasis. "I'll tell you why. He gave up a good import-export business in New York because he was tired of trade restrictions. Because it was all 'import' and no 'export' except raw products. Because—"

"Randall!" The one quiet word from Mother checked her husband. He leaned back in his chair and puffed on his pipe once more.

Randy nodded, his eyes shining. "And when the French threatened he went to war against them."

"That he did. Gave his life at Quebec along with General Wolfe and many another brave Englishman." Father looked at Randy sharply. "Son, are you talking of your grandfather to put off doing your chores?"

19

"No sir. I was thinking about brave men and—and sort of leading up to what happened at school today."

"And what did happen?"

"Master Bundy whipped me."

"Why?"

"He didn't like the speech I gave."

A smile touched the corner of Mr. Stewart's mouth. "Genesis again?"

"No sir. Master Bundy told me to say it for you. This is it." His gaze steady on his father, Randy gave his speech.

For a long moment Mr. Stewart sat quiet, his mouth tightly shut, a strange expression on his face.

"Aren't they wonderful words, Father? Don't they make you want to grab a gun and go fight the—"

"Stop! Hush such talk! Where did you hear those words?"

A loud rap at the door prevented Randy from replying. At a nod from his father he opened it.

A short, heavy-set man, elegantly dressed, his hair powdered and in a queue, stood there. Randy was too startled to speak but his father called a hearty, "Come in, Squire, come in and sit down." He indicated a large, easy chair. "Son, be about your chores."

The squire raised a pudgy hand. "Just a minute, boy! My visit concerns you."

Randy paused uncertainly, then at a nod from his father sat down on the bench again.

Squire Telford bowed to Mrs. Stewart and seated himself. "It has come to my attention," he said, "that Master Bundy was much displeased with your son today, friend Stewart. Much displeased, indeed."

Mr. Stewart nodded, his face serious. "And with good reason, considering the speech he gave. We were about to have a session in the woodshed over it when you came."

"A proper thing to do," approved the squire. He turned to Randy. "Did you not know it was treason you were uttering?"

"No sir." Randy's eyes were round and innocent, his face without expression. "They were high-sounding words. Master Bundy likes phrases which have a grand ring to them."

"Why, he looks and talks as if he had less sense than Dencie," thought Cynthia, amazed, yet relieved.

"You are old enough to give heed to the words you say," Mr. Stewart told his son.

Squire Telford nodded. "In such times as these, even the young must weigh their words carefully. Now—" his tone changed sharply, "where did you learn that speech? Not in your father's house, I warrant."

"Certainly not!" Mr. Stewart said.

"Where did you hear them?" the squire demanded again.

"I took a letter from Father to the post carrier at the tavern," Randy answered. "Some men were at the table eating. One talked so loudly I could not help but hear."

"The tavern is no place for a boy to loiter," Mr. Stewart said.

"I was waiting for the carrier. You told me to put the letter into his hands."

"Ah yes, so I did. It was to a furniture dealer in New York," he explained to his guest. "He desires me to send more chairs like the one in which you are sitting. Says there is a ready sale for them among the British officers."

"A comfortable chair," approved Squire Telford, settling himself more solidly. Then turning to Randy once more, "Who were these men who made such treasonable utterances?"

"Strangers. I had never seen them before."

The squire nodded his satisfaction. "I was sure none of our people were mouthing such treason. We have enjoyed the king's protection to a high degree in our little valley. We will continue to do so as long as we deserve it. But it behooves us to be careful in word, thought and deed. We would not have happen to us what happened at Tazewell Corners."

There was silence for a moment as they thought of the news which had come in the week before. Tazewell Corners, looted and burned. The inhabitants driven out because they were "rebels." They had refused to supply food for the British army.

"That reminds me," the squire said, "of the second part of my mission tonight. The first was to find out about the affair at school, and that I will conclude with a word to the boy here. Do as your father says—think before you speak."

"Yes sir," Randy said. "I will be more thoughtful."

Mrs. Stewart, who had been sewing beside the fireplace, spoke to Cynthia, "Bring some cider, my dear."

Cynthia took the pitcher from the dresser and went across the porch to the buttery. The moonlight was bright on the yard. She paused to admire it, and glimpsed a figure under the big oak. Surprise held her motionless. Whoever it was had not noticed her. He was lifting something. Why, it was Peter Estry! As she looked, he held the object close and started for the fence.

Cynthia dashed off the porch. "Peter," she called. "What are you taking?"

The boy seemed minded to jump the fence and flee. Then he stopped, set down the object and waited for Cynthia.

She burst out laughing when she saw it was the

doll cradle Polly had left out. "You, Peter," she taunted, "wanting a doll cradle!"

"I do not." His snarl was so savage Cynthia drew back. But she said, stoutly, "You were going away with it."

"It is a nice plaything for a little girl," he stammered. He touched it gently with his foot and set it rocking. "With a toy like that, she would stay at home and not run away."

"You mean your little sister?"

Peter turned his face away and mumbled, "She would like one."

"Then make her one. Father made this one for me when I was smaller than Polly."

He didn't answer, but stood gazing across the field.

"Peter," Cynthia asked, "did you tell the squire about Randy's trouble at school?"

He still said nothing and Cynthia went on, "You did. Don't deny it. That's why the squire pays for your schooling—so you can carry tales for him. You're not interested in learning."

"Think what you please," Peter said sullenly. He jumped the fence and started across the field.

Cynthia picked up the cradle and looked at it fondly. "I'll give Polly a scolding for leaving it out," she thought as she carried it back to the porch.

CHAPTER 3

As Cynthia came out of the buttery with the cider, Randy stepped onto the porch. "Sis," he whispered, "I want you to listen to what the squire says and tell me when we go to bed."

"Why don't you stay? You're sure to think I didn't hear right."

"I have to do chores. Listen carefully. Keep your mind on what he is saying."

"I'm not such a dunce as you think I am." Cynthia turned away angrily, then turned back. "Peter Estry was going to steal my doll cradle, but I stopped him."

"Your doll cradle?"

"For his little sister. Do you think the squire brought him?"

"Of course. He's the squire's hired snooper. If I catch him at it I'll make him sorry. Now mind you listen—"

"Sssh!" Cynthia went into the kitchen.

"You took overly long," her father chided. "Did you have to press the apples?"

"There—there was someone lurking by the big

oak," Cynthia stammered. "He went away while I watched."

If the squire knew who the lurker was he made no sign.

"Probably a shadow," her father said. "Girls are fanciful." He poured two mugs of cider and shoved one across the table to his guest. "Wet your whistle. Talking is dry work."

Cynthia got her knitting and seated herself as near the table as she dared.

The squire took a draught of cider. "Prime stuff!" He wiped his mouth with a fine linen handkerchief. "Now about this business of the king I mentioned. You know that however humble and unworthy I may be, I am the king's representative in these parts."

"A most worthy one," Mr. Stewart declared.

"Thank you. Be that as it may, the British are in urgent need of supplies. Traitors have destroyed the supply trains sent up from New York City. It will be necessary for loyal subjects to provide more supplies." He gave Mr. Stewart a sly glance and added, "Naturally, the loyalty of the king's subjects will be measured by their generosity."

Mr. Stewart looked grave. "That is unfortunate for me since I have been away two years and had little harvest."

"I understand. Money would be equally acceptable."

27

"Of money I have even less. I brought not a penny from England with me. 'Wait until the war is over,' they told me."

"Afraid you'd be robbed by the rebels, no doubt. So your trip was fruitless?"

"So far as getting my ancestral estate settled, yes. Of course, it gave me a rare chance to study the war from England's point of view."

The squire wagged his head sadly. "How they must hate us! Ingratitude—rebellion—treason."

"On the contrary, it is surprising how much sympathy there is for the—the rebels." Father seemed to choke a bit and took a drink of cider.

The squire's eyes popped. "Sympathy for the rebels? How can that be?"

"A matter of trade, possibly. Their trade has fallen off as badly as ours. People are touchiest where their pocketbooks are concerned."

"True. But can't they see it would be quickest cured by subduing the rebellion?" Squire Telford took a memorandum from his pocket and studied it. "I have a fair supply of meal promised, also honey and vegetables."

"I will donate a sack of dried apples," Mother said. "And ham—we can spare a ham or two and a flitch of bacon, can we not, Randall?"

Her husband nodded. "Fetch the squire a pen, daughter."

Cynthia brought a quill pen and the ink stand.

Squire Telford jotted down the items. "A shoat?" he asked. "Perhaps a lamb or two? Better to donate a few than have them all commandeered, eh, friend Stewart?"

"I have few swine," Mr. Stewart said. "However, I will give one, and two lambs. Never let it be said that Randall Stewart is niggardly in such a good cause."

"A man after my own heart!" approved the squire. "Have these things at the tavern Thursday next. They are to be taken as speedily as possible to the British lines."

"How can they get past Fort Ticonderoga and Fort Edward?"

"Secret trails known only to Indians." The squire emptied his mug and rose. "I mustn't keep you from your appointment with your son."

Mr. Stewart escorted his guest to the door and wished him good night. As the squire's steps receded from the porch, he gave his wife a long look. "So the looters have come over the hill," he muttered. "I had hoped—"

"Cynthia," her mother interrupted firmly, "please take Polly to bed. The poor child is asleep on the rug."

Before Cynthia could do so, Randy came in. "The squire left Peter to spy on you," he told his father. "So you had better beat me hard."

Mr. Stewart's face flushed. "Are you sure?"

Randy nodded. "Peter was lurking behind the barn while I did the chores. I pretended not to see him. I met Squire Telford as I was coming to the house. I slipped back after him just for fun. Peter started home with him, but the squire stopped him. He's hiding behind the woodshed now. No doubt he'll count the strokes of the whip."

"Come," said his father gruffly, "let's get it over with so Peter can go home to bed."

Cynthia forgot she was to take Polly to bed. Mother seemed to have forgotten it too. She folded her sewing and put it in a drawer of the dresser. She stood tense and still for a moment, then seized a broom and began to sweep the hearth.

There came a loud sound from the woodshed. She threw down the broom and clenched her hands. "Poor Randall!" she groaned. "Poor man!"

"Poor Randy, you mean," Cynthia said.

Her mother paid no attention but muttered something which sounded like, "How long, oh Lord, how long?"

The heavy blows came regularly now, punctuated by an occasional howl from Randy.

"Stop him, Mother, stop him!" begged Cynthia. "Father never made Randy yell before."

"Take Polly to bed." Mother's face was white.

There came an extra loud cry from Randy. With a squeal almost as loud, Cynthia threw herself into her mother's arms. They clung together while from the woodshed came the sound of Mr. Stewart's voice, loud and harsh.

There were no more blows. Presently the door opened and Randy limped in. He averted his face and hurried to the stairs.

Mr. Stewart entered behind him. "Say good night properly to your mother," he ordered.

Randy still held his face averted. "Good night, Mother," he muttered.

His mother threw her arms about him and kissed him. "You'll be more careful after this, won't you, dear?" she said.

"*Yes ma'am!*" With a muttered, "Good night, Father," Randy scuttled upstairs.

Cynthia kissed her mother and bestowed a cool peck on her father's cheek. She lifted Polly from the rug and guided her stumbling feet up the stairs.

Randy was at the window in her room looking out into the moonlit yard. "Wanted to be sure that snooper had gone home to report," he said. "Guess he has. I can't see him. Wait till I catch him in the woods again, just you wait."

"He's smaller than you are. You won't do anything to him," Cynthia answered, unbuttoning Polly's shoes.

"No, I guess not. Anyway, I promised Father I wouldn't."

To Cynthia's surprise he began to chuckle. She

stopped with Polly's stocking half off. "Whatever have you got to laugh at, Randy Stewart?"

His chuckles increased. "If you knew, Sis—if you only knew!"

"Well, tell me. I need to hear something funny."

With only a "Good night" he went to his room.

Cynthia heard Polly drowsily murmur her prayers. She got herself ready for bed, all the time wondering what had made Randy laugh. Finally, she wrapped a robe about her and tiptoed into his room. "Randy," she whispered, "I want to tell you something."

"Won't it keep until morning?"

"You asked me to listen so I could tell you what the squire said."

Randy sat up. "Go ahead."

Cynthia told him how the squire had solicited supplies for the British, and what their parents were going to donate.

"Our food, going to feed those murderers!" he groaned.

"Father called them 'looters,'" Cynthia said.

"Looters? You sure? Tell me just what he said."

Cynthia sat for a moment trying to remember. "It was after the squire went. Father stood against the door. He looked tired. He said to Mother, 'So the looters have come over the hill. I had hoped—'"

"Go on—go on."

33

"Let me see. Oh, Mother told me to take Polly to bed. You came in and told about Peter—"

"'I had hoped—'" Randy repeated the words thoughtfully. "What do you suppose he had hoped? That the British would stay away from Beaver Valley? Or—" eagerness crept into his voice—"did he hope that the patriots would drive them back into Canada? Could he—does he hope that?"

"I don't know. I told you what he said and what the squire said. Now tell me why you laughed."

"I can't," Randy began, then stopped. "You did a good job of reporting, though." He was silent for a moment. "Sis, give me your right hand." He interlocked his fingers in hers. It was their symbol of secrecy. "Now promise you won't tell."

"I promise." Cynthia was a little breathless as always with the solemnity of the pledge.

Randy released her hand. "Father was beating the sawhorse, not me."

"The sawhorse? But you yelled."

"He told me to, so Peter would hear and have something to tell."

"Didn't Father whip you at all?"

"Nary a touch. He was mad because the squire left Peter to check on him. He said we'd give him plenty to report. I'd like to be a mouse in the wall and hear what he tells the squire."

"You wouldn't dare. You'd giggle," Cynthia said,

giggling herself. After a moment, she jumped up and started for the stairs.

"What are you going to do?" Randy demanded.

"Going to give Father a big hug. I couldn't when I said good night."

"Come back here. You promised."

"I won't tell."

"He'd know. He wouldn't like it if he knew I told you."

"Why?"

"Because it's too important. If the squire found out, he'd make trouble for Father."

"I wish Mother knew," sighed Cynthia. "She was so unhappy."

"I think Father'll tell her." Randy laughed. "If she makes griddlecakes for breakfast we'll know he told her. She makes them when she is happy. Good night, Sis." He burrowed into the covers.

Cynthia went back to her own bed feeling much happier.

CHAPTER 4

The griddle was heating and Mother was busy stirring batter when the children came downstairs next morning. Randy gave his sister a grin as he went out to milk.

Cynthia started to dress Polly, but she pulled away. "I'm a big girl now," she said. "I can dress myself. Yesterday I climbed the fence and found some pretty flowers. Today—"

"Today you will get spanked hard if you go outside the yard," Mother said. "Little maids of four are not to go into the woods alone. But it is fine if you can dress yourself. Then big sister can fill the oven for me. This is baking day."

"Goody!" exclaimed Cynthia. She left Polly to dress herself and went to the woodshed for oven sticks. The large brick oven was at one side of the fireplace. It would be filled with wood and heated thoroughly. Then the coals would be raked out and the oven filled with bread, pies and cakes.

For lesser baking, Mother used the baking kettle, an iron pot with legs. It could be placed in the coals for heating. It had a deep lid into which coals could be piled. Besides using it for stews and dumplings,

Mother made hot bread and puddings in it. The great oven was heated once a week.

"More shavings, daughter," Mrs. Stewart said. "Spread them far to the back so the fire is even. There is a great trick to heating an oven properly. Use the shovel so you won't soil your sleeves. Now the coals, far back. Then plenty of light wood."

"I'd learn housework quicker if I didn't have to go to school," Cynthia said, carefully laying the wood as Mother directed.

"We have been over that before," Mother answered. "Your father and I agree that girls need education as well as boys." She sighed. "Your poor father! If only he could have stayed at Harvard! He loves knowledge. Since he can't get more for himself, it is his dearest wish for his children to have it."

"He left Harvard when his father was killed, didn't he?"

"Yes. His mother and two sisters were left alone on this place. So he came home like a dutiful son and cared for them."

"It's fine for Randy to have some book learning, but I don't need it." Cynthia returned to her argument. "Dencie and I are the only girls in school. The squire sends Dencie because she hasn't any mother to teach her at home. I don't think she has learned one thing at school."

"Well, you have. I can't say I'm proud of the

way you do sums, but your copybook is neat and you read the Bible right well."

"Oh, do you think so, Mother?" Cynthia glowed at the words of praise.

Randy came in from milking then, and Mother said, "Randy, put the big wood in the oven now. Cynthia has a good fire started. Daughter, get the milk strained."

After straining the milk into crocks and setting it in the cool buttery, Cynthia helped Polly. She had put her dress on hind side before. By the time it was straightened and her curls brushed, breakfast was ready.

There was little talking at breakfast. Mrs. Stewart kept the plates filled while the others enjoyed the tender brown cakes swimming in maple syrup.

"That will be enough griddlecakes for me," Mr. Stewart announced at last. "If you will excuse me, my dear, I'll get along to work. Mind you children learn your lessons today."

As he rose from the table, Randy said, "Father, I want to tell you one thing about last night—"

"It's over and done with and you have promised to guard your tongue in the future." Mr. Stewart did not check his stride toward the door.

"I didn't learn that speech at the tavern," blurted Randy.

His father stopped abruptly. "Where, then?"

"In the woods. I was alone. An old man with white hair and a bad limp came by."

Mr. Stewart cast a quick look at his wife. "What did he say? Tell me all."

"He said he was 'a voice crying in the wilderness.'"

"Why did you not tell me this sooner?"

"I had no chance. The squire came."

"What else did he say? Think back carefully."

Randy hesitated. "He was a kind old man and he believed the things he told me. I would not have harm come to him through me. Cynthia, you won't tell Dencie or anyone? Promise?"

"Of course I promise," Cynthia said. And Polly echoed, "So do I."

The others smiled and Randy said, "First off, he asked me if the Stewart place was near. Said he'd been a comrade of Captain Randall Stewart in the French and Indian war. I told him where our place was, and who I was. He asked me what I was doing in the woods and I said I was getting wood for the schoolmaster's fire. He asked me about school and Master Bundy, and said to learn all I could as there was great need of educated people. Then he told me the words that I recited at school. 'Is life so dear, or peace so sweet—'"

"Yes, yes. What else?"

"Nothing much. Oh, one thing funny. He said to tell you acorns will ripen early this fall."

40

Mr. Stewart gave a little start, then said, "Some superstition of the season no doubt. Old folks are full of them. Is that all?"

"There was one thing more." Randy looked up, his eyes alight. "After he had told me those words and had me say them back to him, he said, 'Don't forget them, boy. Let them ring in your mind like a bell. Liberty or death, one or the other. Men have to choose.'"

"Let them ring in your mind, but not on your tongue after this," Mr. Stewart said. "The squire's visit showed you why, didn't it?"

Randy nodded. "Then the old man said goodbye and God bless me and he hoped we'd meet under brighter skies, sometime."

"Amen to that!" exclaimed Mother.

"Aye, we all hope for better times soon," agreed Father. With his hand on the door latch he asked, "Did you tell Master Bundy of this man?"

"No. He didn't ask me and I wouldn't have told him. Not if he'd beat me as hard as you did last night." Randy grinned impishly.

His father went out with no further words. Mother leaned down to turn a griddlecake, her dimple in plain sight.

Presently brother and sister were on their way to school, lunchbags in hand. "Dencie will have on a fresh pinafore," Cynthia said, smoothing her own crisp ruffles. "She has a different one each day. Mine must last three days."

"Yes, and who keeps them clean for her? That old lame housekeeper who can scarcely walk. Would you have Mother work that hard?"

"Of course not. I could do my own if I didn't have to go to school. I can starch and iron."

"You wouldn't get to wear your fine starched pinafore every day if you didn't go to school. And you'd have on your linsey-woolsey instead of that fancy dress."

Cynthia hadn't thought of that. Maybe going to school wasn't so bad after all. And it was lovely in the woods with the birds singing and the breeze so balmy.

"What a morning!" she said. "It makes me want to sing. Doesn't it make you feel happy, Randy?"

"Huh?" Randy asked, his thoughts far away.

"This is a morning to be happy. Can't you—"

"I'll tell you what would make me happy, Sis— so happy I'd almost burst with pride. To have our father be Captain Randall Stewart in a buff and blue—" abruptly he checked his words. "See," he said, "every time I open my mouth something comes out that shouldn't. I'll shut my lips and say no more."

"A good idea," agreed Cynthia.

Though he said no more, Randy was busy thinking. He would indeed be proud to see his father in

42

a captain's uniform and mounted upon their high-spirited colt, Ginger, a sword by his side. For two years Father had worn a patriot's uniform and been with Washington while the squire and all Beaver Crossing had thought he was in England getting his inheritance.

Those had been hard days for the Stewarts, pretending Father was across the ocean when he was only a few hundred miles away. Now, with Father home, and not in uniform, it was harder than ever, for he was posing as a good Tory. Instead, he was gathering information which would be valuable to Washington.

"This is more dangerous than fighting in battle," he had told his wife and son. "Dangerous not only for me but for all of us. That is why we must be most careful in what we do and say."

"If it is so dangerous, why didn't you stay with General Washington?" Randy had asked.

"Because I can best serve my country here," Mr. Stewart had explained. "The British are coming down from Canada. General Washington must be kept informed of their progress and number. Who so fitted to do it as one who belongs here? My general asked me to come and I came. I am proud to be of service to him."

Randy was proud, too. "I'll help," he declared. "I'll find out all I can, and—"

"Your part is to be a good Tory's son," his father

said, emphatically. "You ask no questions. You know nothing if asked. You make no talk of war. That way we stay out of trouble. Do you understand?"

Randy nodded, thinking it was a poor part to play, yet realizing the wisdom of his father's words.

Now, remembering his folly of yesterday, he groaned. How could he have been so silly! How fortunate they got out of it so nicely! Never, never again would he be so careless!

"What are you looking for, Sis?" he asked Cynthia who was looking first on one side of the path, then on the other. "Lost something? Or do you expect to find diamonds?"

"Daisies." Cynthia stopped to pick one. "If I get enough, Dencie and I will make daisy chains at the noon hour."

"Daisy chains!" snorted Randy in deep disgust.

Cynthia found plenty of daisies, but there was no noon hour. Master Bundy made them go on working sums while they ate their sandwiches.

"You must work hard today," he said. "Because I am going to let school out for two weeks." He scowled at the murmur of delight which swept the room. "I would not have a vacation at this time if my corn did not need weeding. Knowledge is important; so is food. The British coming down from Canada need supplies. We must raise all we can.

44

You boys who are big enough, get into the fields during vacation."

Cynthia started home happy that night. Two weeks without school! She would help Mother with the soap-making and dyeing. Maybe they would dye some blue cloth for a new dress for her.

"Vacation so he can raise food for the British!" fumed Randy. "I hope it rots in the ground! I hope they starve!"

"I won't listen to any more of your wild talk. You can walk home by yourself." Cynthia dashed down a side path which led home in a more round-about way. It was rough and she soon wished she hadn't come. She would not turn back, though. If Randy didn't have her to talk to, maybe he wouldn't say those awful things which could get him into trouble.

It was quiet on the path. There wasn't even a bird song. The stillness was broken suddenly, but not by a song. Cynthia stopped, startled. The sound came again.

CHAPTER 5

As the sound came again Cynthia turned and fled. She had scarcely breath left to call Randy.

He looked back and grinned. "My, what scared little sister? Was it a big, black bear?"

"Randy, someone's hurt."

"Who?"

"I didn't see. I heard them moan terribly."

"Probably Peter Estry wanting to frighten you."

"It was *not* Peter Estry. Someone is hurt. If you won't go back with me, I'll go alone. They have to have help." She started back along the path.

Randy hesitated. "Where was it?"

"By the quarry."

"There's a short cut." Randy plunged into the woods and Cynthia followed. "I still think it's Peter," he said. "We'll take him by surprise coming this way. Be quiet."

Cynthia was sure it was not Peter, but she did not argue. Presently she whispered, "There, in that little hollow—that's where I heard it."

Randy pulled her behind a bush. "Wait here while I look." Stealthily he advanced to a big rock and peered from behind it into the hollow. A moment later he beckoned Cynthia and went around the rock.

Cynthia, hurrying after him, saw a crumpled form lying on the ground. A ray of sunlight shone on his white hair. "Is it the old man?" she asked.

Randy nodded. "What's the matter, sir?" he asked, bending over the figure. A moan was the only answer.

"Poor man! Shall I run and get Father?" Cynthia asked.

"No. Get some water." Randy snatched off his felt hat and gave it to her. He took a wizened wrist in his hand and was relieved to feel a steady though slow pulse.

Cynthia came back with water. Randy bathed the old man's forehead and wrists and moistened his lips.

The eyelids opened a slit. "Water," the man mumbled. "Give me a drink."

Randy lifted the white head gently. He folded the hat so that water from one corner ran into the man's mouth.

He drank deeply, then waved the water away. "Good! I have been wanting that all day."

"What happened?" Randy asked.

"Men from the tavern knocked me over the ledge."

Cynthia looked at the high ledge and shuddered.

"Any bones broken?" Randy asked.

47

"Naught except my ankle. It is either broken or badly sprained. My head hurts where I bumped it on a rock."

Randy noticed blood on the snowy hair. "Even then you got off lucky," he said.

"I did indeed."

"You'll have to be taken to some comfortable place. Ours is nearest. Cynthia, go get Father—"

"I cannot go to your house. There's a fissure here in the old quarry where I have stayed many times. It will do. Bind my ankle and help me there. Could you do that, lad?"

"Please come to our house," Randy begged. "Father is—" he paused, not daring to say what was in his mind. "Father will not let harm come to you."

"I cannot go to your house." The man's tone checked Randy. "If you don't want to help me—"

"Oh, we do, we do. If you only knew Father better. And Mother is a prime nurse."

"I have no doubt. Maybe some day I shall know them. If you will pull off my right boot—gently, lad, gently."

Even the slight pull Randy gave caused the man's face to turn ashen and a moan escaped his tightly-pressed lips.

"We'll have to cut the boot," Randy said. The old man nodded.

Randy took his clasp knife and carefully slit the boot, thankful that it was old worn leather. He re-

49

moved it, disclosing a red, swollen ankle. "Now we need a bandage. How about your apron, Sis?"

"My—my apron? You mean tear it up?" Cynthia looked at her pretty pinafore in dismay. "It's one of my best."

Randy continued to hold out his hand. She sighed and said, "Well, if you really need it." She started to untie the strings, then stopped. Her face flushed, but she smiled. "I'll get you a better bandage. Wait a minute." She ran behind a bush and ripped a ruffle from one of her petticoats. "Here." She handed it to Randy. "I wish it wasn't starched, but it's long and quite clean."

"Fine." Randy rolled the cloth into a compact ball. "While I bandage his leg, you look around for Peter. We don't want him snooping."

Cynthia made a wide circuit around the quarry and found no sign of Peter. "He isn't around," she reported.

"Good." Randy straightened up and looked with pride at the bandage he had made. "Now we're ready for the head."

"A fistful of cobwebs would fix the sore on my head fine," said the old man. "Are there any on the bushes?"

They looked, but could find none, so Randy washed the starch from a piece of the ruffle and bound the man's head. "You look like a soldier back from the wars," he said, laughing.

The old man's eyes flashed. "It's too soon to come back from the wars. With Burgoyne and his troops coming down from the north and St. Leger with his red hordes coming from the west."

"Have you been—have you seen—" Randy began eagerly.

The old man interrupted, "No time nor place to tell of where I've been. Get me to that shelter, lad. First things first."

"All right." Randy tried not to show his disappointment. "Let's get you in marching order. How are we going to do it? Sis, you help on his good side. I'll take the other. Don't put any weight on that foot, sir. Lean on me and hobble. Lean heavy, I'm strong."

The man's face was white with pain before they got him erect, his arm across Randy's shoulder.

"A blessing it was my lame leg got sprained," he said. "Had it been my good one, I'd have been in a real pother. To the right," he said a moment later. "Veer to the right a bit."

The going was rough through the rubble of the quarry. The old man's forehead was wet with perspiration. He breathed so hard it frightened Randy. "Shall we stop a minute?" he asked. "Maybe you need another drink."

"Go on, go on." The voice was a mere thread. "It's close. See, there's the place."

Randy looked at the opening in the rock. "That's

a dangerous place. Father told us never to go in there because of rock falls."

A faint smile touched the old man's lips. "Safer for me if folks are a-scared."

They helped him through the crevice and into a space large enough for a man to lie down in. "Lean on Cynthia for a little," Randy said. "I'll get some boughs for a bed."

"No. You two get along home." The man lowered himself carefully to the ground. "Fetch me a blanket if you can later."

"I will tonight, and food. Is there anything else?"

"No." Then as they turned away he called, "Oh, yes. I must have a piece of birch bark. Better get it now."

Randy quickly got a piece and the children started home. "Sis," he said, when they had gone a short distance, "let's not tell Father about the old man."

"Why not? You know how Father feels."

"He might get into trouble. I think that's why the old man wouldn't come to our house. Father's work is so important that nothing must endanger it. We'll take care of him ourselves. That will be our way of helping Father."

"All right," Cynthia agreed. "It'll be hard for me to keep still, though. I'm not used to having secrets from Father and Mother."

"Try hard," Randy said. "Remember it will help Father. Now come on *fast*. We're late."

"They'll ask why we were so late," Cynthia gasped, trying to keep up with his long-legged trot.

"That's right." Randy looked about the woods for something of interest. He pointed to a grassy glade. "Strawberries are ripe. We'll take Polly some."

Swiftly they picked handfuls of the luscious little berries, not stopping to eat any.

"Tomorrow," vowed Cynthia, "I'm coming out and eat my fill."

"Mother will think we took plenty of time to eat our fill tonight," laughed Randy. "Here, put these in your pocket and come on."

"You'll have to get food ready for me to take to the old man," he said as they raced along.

"How can I? What—"

"Some meat and bread, stuff I can easily carry and Mother won't miss. Wrap it up and put it in a corner of the buttery where I can find it."

"How will you go without their knowing?"

"I'll climb out the window and go down the oak tree after they're asleep."

"Oh, dear," sighed Cynthia. "It would have been so much simpler if we could have brought him to the house."

"Simpler? Suppose the squire had found out

he was there? What do you think would happen to the old man—and to us?"

Cynthia shuddered at her brother's serious tone. "I'll be glad when it is over and George Washington is king," she said.

No more was said until they came in sight of home. Then Randy exclaimed, "Oh-oh, Father's unharnessing Maje already. It's later than I thought. I'll fetch a big armload of wood. That ought to help."

Cynthia hurried into the kitchen. The candles were lighted and the table set. Mother was busy at the fireplace and didn't turn around.

Cynthia made her voice as light and gay as she could. "Who wants something good?"

"I do, I do," shrilled Polly who was laying spoons at the table.

"Feel in my pocket." Cynthia wished that her mother would turn around or say something. "They're strawberries, pet. They're good. Try one." As Polly only fingered them, she added, "Don't you remember last year when we picked them on the hill?"

"Oh yes, I remember." Polly began eating the berries.

"They're going to be thick," Cynthia said to her mother, whose back was still turned. "I think we can get plenty for preserves."

"Run along and change quickly. Your father will be in soon." Mother still didn't turn.

"No more school for two weeks," Randy said at supper. His father looked up surprised and Randy added, "Master Bundy has to hoe his corn."

"Ah," was all Father said.

"Mother, will you make soap while we have our vacation?" Cynthia asked. "I love making soap."

"Perhaps. I have some sewing to do for Polly first. She has outgrown all her dresses."

"I could help you with that, too. You said yourself that I make neat stitches."

"I will see that you have plenty to do," Mother said. "For a starter, you may do the dishes alone since you were so late in getting home." She turned to Polly. "I'll tell you that story you've been wanting."

Immediately after supper Father went to bed, saying he was tired from a hard day in the field. "I'll have you help me with the haying tomorrow," he told Randy. "So see that you get up promptly."

With Mother telling stories to Polly in the chimney corner, it was easy for Cynthia to pack a parcel of food and slip it into the buttery.

As soon as the chores were done, Randy followed his father's example and went to bed. On the way he whispered to Cynthia, "Wake me when you come to bed."

She didn't have to, she found, after she had tucked Polly into bed. He was lying fully dressed and wide-eyed.

"I couldn't sleep," he said. "Things kept going around in my head. Burgoyne coming down the Hudson, St. Leger and his Indians from the west."

"Don't talk about Indians at night," quavered Cynthia.

"We're in no danger in this valley," Randy said. "Don't think about your precious self so much when brave men are fighting and dying to make a free country."

"George Washington will be king when the patriots win, won't he? He'd look fine in a crown."

"Hush!" growled Randy. "Do you want to wake Father? Did you fix the food?"

"Yes, and I put a jug by it so you could take him some water."

Randy chuckled. "I'll fill it with cider. Get a blanket, will you, Sis?"

Cynthia selected a well-worn one which her mother wouldn't mind losing too much. She handed it to Randy after he was in the tree. "Be careful, oh, do be careful," she whispered, suddenly afraid to let him go.

"Don't worry about me." His tone showed he was enjoying himself.

Cynthia watched until he had slid down the trunk, then hurried to her own window. She heard

Tip making a questioning sound and knew Randy had gone into the buttery. She saw him come out and disappear, sending Tip back with a wave of his hand.

She sat at the window following in her mind's eye Randy's path through the woods. Her imagination peopled it with dangers—a bear—a prowling Indian, or worst of all, Peter Estry spying for the squire. For relief, she turned to thoughts of George Washington as king. He would live in New York, of course. Maybe she could be lady-in-waiting to Queen Martha. She dozed off on this pleasant thought.

She woke, cramped and chilly. The moon was out of sight. She must have slept for hours. Randy was probably in bed. As she rose to go and see, a movement in the dusky yard caught her eye. There he was now. But what was he doing? He seemed to be going away from the house instead of toward it. Why, it wasn't Randy. The figure was as large as Father's. She watched the man disappear into the barn. She hurried into Randy's room. The bed was empty.

CHAPTER 6

Cynthia stood beside Randy's empty bed trembling with terror. Randy not there and a prowler in the yard! She went to the window and looked into the oak tree. It was empty. There was only one thing to do—tell Father. Even now the intruder might be setting fire to the barn or stealing a horse. She hurried downstairs and over to the bedroom door. About to open it, she stopped. What should she tell them about Randy? Nothing, of course. She'd say she saw someone prowling.

But what if Father went out to look, and Randy came? She stood still, uncertain what to do. Finally, she tiptoed to the porch and looked at the shadowy outline of the barn. Everything seemed peaceful. Tip gave a welcoming thump of his tail, and she wondered why he hadn't barked at the prowler. Could she have been mistaken about seeing someone? She took a step into the yard, then shrank back at the sight of a hurrying figure.

Before she could scream or move, he was out of sight around the corner of the house. She realized that this was really Randy and hurried after him.

He was already shinning up the oak. "Randy," she whispered, "wait. It's me, Cynthia."

He slid down and whispered angrily, "What are you doing out here, silly?"

"There's a man in the barn. I saw him go across the yard. We ought to tell Father."

"You sure?" Randy stood in thought for a moment. "I'll go look. If there's any need, I'll call Father." He gave her a push toward the porch. "Go back to bed."

Cynthia stood on the porch and watched Randy fade into the darkness. She stared at the dark blot which was the barn and wondered what was happening. She wished she had gone with Randy and was minded to follow him.

The brooding stillness held her inactive even while it filled her with terror. I'll count to a thousand, she thought. Then if Randy isn't back, I'll call Father.

But terrible things could happen to Randy while she counted. She ran across the kitchen and threw open the bedroom door. "Father," she said, "wake up! There's someone at the barn. Randy's gone to look. I'm scared."

It was her mother's voice which answered. She didn't sound sleepy, but startled. "Randy at the barn? I must get him."

"Where is Father?"

Mother didn't answer. She pulled a robe over her gown and hurried out-of-doors. "Go back to bed," she ordered over her shoulder.

Cynthia had had all the watching from afar that she could stand. She pattered after her mother.

Halfway across the yard, Mother stopped. There were voices at the barn door. Two indistinct shadows appeared and grew more distinct as they approached. Randy and Father!

At the sight of his womenfolks, Father stopped short. "What in time!" he exclaimed.

"Cynthia was frightened and called me," Mrs. Stewart explained.

"A fine to-do!" he growled. "I can't go out to see Snorter without the whole family trailing me!" He said no more but stamped into the house. The others followed silently.

Snorter, the old red bull! So that's what had taken Father out into the night. Relief made Cynthia want to laugh but she thought she had better not. Once upstairs, she fell on Randy's bed and giggled. "If that isn't the funniest! I never thought of it's being Father. I might have known, though, because Tip didn't bark."

"The funny thing to me," Randy said, "is how quiet Snorter was. Critters mostly bawl when they are sick. And tending him in the dark, too. Not a bit of light, then suddenly here's Father coming out of the barn. He almost ran over me. And the way he grabbed me! I thought he'd choke me before I could say who I was."

"What did you tell him?"

"I said you saw someone and I came to look. He said next time to call him first thing."

"Mother must have known what Father was doing. Why didn't she tell me? And why did she go out?"

"Hmm! I don't know unless she feared I would bother Father. Snorter is so touchy. When I first went out there, I climbed into the harness room through the back window. I was standing there wondering what to do when I heard voices, muffled-like. I couldn't tell where they came from."

"Father talking to Snorter?"

"Snorter wouldn't answer. I heard two voices. I think Father had a meeting with someone out there. I wish he wouldn't treat me like a child."

Cynthia yawned. "I think you imagined it. I'm going to bed. Oh, was the old man all right?"

"Yes. I got boughs and made him a bed. He liked the cider and said there was food enough for two days. He told me not to come near tomorrow. He's afraid someone will find he's hiding there. He had me deliver a message."

"Randy, you shouldn't have! That was dangerous."

"No, it wasn't. All I did was put a piece of birch

bark with marks on it in a certain place. I don't know who'll get it or what the marks meant."

"Sounds silly to me." Cynthia started for her room.

"Silly, is it?" Randy grabbed his sister by the wrist. "Listen, I'll tell you how silly it is. The British are trying to cut us in two."

"Cu—cut us in two?" gasped Cynthia.

"The colonies, I mean. General Burgoyne is coming from the North, St. Leger from the West, Howe from the South. They aim to meet at Albany."

"Albany? That's not far from here."

"No. New York will be cut off from New England and from the Southern colonies. Divided that way—"

"Children," came a stern call from below, "be quiet at once!"

Cynthia fled to her room. She had no more than got into bed when a cautious voice whispered in her ear, "The old man says we mustn't let it happen. He says we've all got to help."

Cynthia shoved her brother away and pulled the covers over her head. Her dreams the rest of the night were haunted by a red-coated figure brandishing a sword and threatening to cut her in two.

At breakfast her father asked, "Daughter, how was it you saw me go into the barn at midnight?"

The question caught her unprepared. "Why," she stammered, "I—I—" She glanced at Randy who scowled warningly at her. She swallowed and began again, "The moonlight was pretty. I went to sleep at the window. When I woke up I saw someone. I was scared. I didn't know it was you."

Mother shook her head. "Silly child! Have you no regard for your health?"

"Do your sleeping in bed after this," her father said. "Snorter is better this morning, so let's put it out of our minds and say nothing to anyone about the matter." He looked from one to the other of the children and repeated, "Nothing, remember." They nodded, impressed by his gravity.

He went on in a lighter tone, "Well, son, we must get into the hayfield or Snorter and the other animals will starve this winter."

He was busy with the scythe and Randy was raking hay into windrows when Master Bundy came hurrying out of the woods. Randy was surprised. The schoolmaster had never visited them.

"Master Bundy's coming," he said, hoping he was not the cause of the visit.

Father checked his scythe in mid-air. "What in time!" he muttered. He lowered his scythe and leaned on it, waiting for the visitor to come closer.

"My flail," panted Master Bundy, making no pretense of greeting. "I broke it. May I borrow yours?"

64

"Your flail?" blurted Randy. "I thought you were going to hoe corn."

The schoolmaster flung him an impatient look. "I have also a field of grain," he snapped. He turned back to Father, and it seemed to Randy that some unspoken message flashed from his eyes. That was nonsense, though. They didn't know each other. Master Bundy had come to Beaver Crossing only a few months ago, while Father was away. They couldn't have met or Father would have mentioned it.

Mr. Stewart's voice was distant, but courteous as to any stranger as he said, "Certainly you may borrow it. Go fetch it, Randy. And while you are about it, ask your mother for a cool drink for the gentleman. He looks fair winded."

Randy threw down his rake gladly and set off for the house, thankful that Master Bundy had not come about school matters. He poked his head into the kitchen. "Father wants a cool drink for Master Bundy," he said. "Shall I take buttermilk or cider?"

"Master Bundy?" Mother's voice was shrill with surprise. "You mean he's here?"

"Yes, he came to borrow a flail."

Mrs. Stewart stood staring at the floor, her forehead wrinkled.

"Which shall I take, buttermilk or—"

"Cider, of course." Mother stepped quickly to the door. "I'll take it myself. He rarely visits us."

As Randy started off the porch she said, "Bring some wood. Your father won't need you for a bit."

"I filled the—"

"Put on more. Pile it up. And—and draw water to fill the tub."

Randy stared at his mother, amazed at her sharp tone. He brought a load of wood and dumped it on the already filled box. "Well," he exclaimed to Cynthia who was on her hands and knees scrubbing the hearth, "Master Bundy excites Mother like he does you and Dencie. She fairly flew out there to take him some cider."

Cynthia straightened up. "You don't think he'll come to the house, do you? I look a sight."

"So does he," Randy laughed. "He's got on old trousers and a faded shirt and his hair is tied back careless. Guess I'll have to get back. You'll have to draw the water."

"What water?"

"Mother wants the tub filled."

"Why? We aren't going to wash."

"I don't know why. She told me to fill it."

"Then you'll have to fill it—not I."

"Father gave me orders first." Randy bounced out the door before Cynthia could answer. As he carried the flail to the meadow he noted with surprise that no one was drinking cider. Mother held the jug unheeded in her hand. All three were grouped together talking earnestly. Once again he wondered uneasily if they were discussing his conduct at school. He thought back, but could remember nothing except the speech, and Father knew about that.

A sudden thought startled him. Had they found out about the old man? No, Master Bundy would go to the squire, not to Father about that. Well, there was only one way to find out what they were talking about. He squared his shoulders and started across the meadow whistling a little tune to show how much at ease he was.

CHAPTER 7

Randy saw his mother glance over her shoulder, then hand the jug to Master Bundy who tipped it high and took a great draught. When Randy came close, the schoolmaster was remarking what good cider it was.

Father said, "Come, Master Bundy, we'll look at the bull if you please. Randy can carry on here. He's a good man with a scythe."

Randy glowed with pride at his father's praise, but looked after the two men, puzzled, as they strode away. "Funny he'd bother Master Bundy about old Snorter when he's in such a hurry," he said.

"He needs advice," Mother answered. "Would you like a sip of cider before you start work?"

Randy took a sizable sip, then picked up the scythe and went to work. He'd show Master Bundy that father was right in calling him a good man with a scythe.

It was half an hour later when Master Bundy strode back to the hay meadow. "Your father will be here presently." He flung the words at Randy in an absent-minded way, and shouldering the flail, hurried away.

As Randy worked, he thought of the things the old man had whispered to him the night before. He could feel yet the hard grasp of bony fingers on his wrist and hear the urgency in the old man's hiss, "The lobster-backs are coming down on Fort Ti thicker'n skeeters in a swamp. They've got to be stopped." He had chuckled as he told how the patriots had scared the Tories away from their farms on the east side of the Hudson. "Skedaddled to Canada, lock, stock and barrel. Good riddance, too. Hope they never come back."

If only we were on the east side of the river, thought Randy. You could dare to be a patriot there without fear of having your home plundered or your scalp lifted. Still, that would change if the British advanced much farther. Maybe they were as well off on the west side of the Hudson. In truth, there was no safety anywhere until the patriots had won.

It was a comfort that they were so far from St. Leger's line of march down the Mohawk. The old man said he was bringing Indians with him. Nobody thought he'd be able to control them once they got started. Two rugged ranges of hills and dense, unsettled forest lay between Beaver Crossing and the Mohawk. Indians would stay where settlers were thicker. Randy shuddered thinking of the settlements which lay open to attack once St. Leger got past Fort Stanwix.

"He's not past there yet, though," Randy remembered. The old man thought there was a chance he wouldn't take the fort. Randy wished the minister would say a prayer for Fort Stanwix on Sunday, instead of "God save the king."

"You and your sister will have to do the haying," Father told Randy at dinner time. "I have to go away."

"Away?" Randy asked hopefully. "You going to join—"

"I am going to take the chairs I have finished over to the river. If I can get them to New York, the British will pay a good price for them."

"How will you get there?" Randy demanded. "Don't the patriots hold the river down past the Mohawk?"

"The rebels, you mean," his father corrected sternly. "As I understand it, they're not interfering with river trade too much. The boat captain I have in mind knows which side his bread is buttered on. He will get them there safely."

"You're not going clear to New York, are you, Father?" Cynthia asked. "I like to have you home."

"I want you home," echoed Polly anxiously.

Father gave his daughters a reassuring smile.

"I'll not be gone long, not more than three nights at most. And with big brother here to tend to things—" His smile vanished. He looked sternly at Randy. "One thing, son, you must guard your tongue. A slip to the squire like the one you made to me about 'patriots' could cause us great trouble."

Randy flushed. "It's only honest to talk as you feel."

"It's only common sense not to get your family into trouble. Which do you consider more important, mouthing words which accomplish naught but trouble or leaving them unsaid for the sake of your mother and sisters? Which? I must know before I go away and leave them in your care."

"I—why, I'll take care of Mother and the girls. You know I will."

Father nodded in satisfaction at Randy's earnest tone. "I knew I could depend on you. Stay close to home. Stay out of arguments. Mother, of course, will be in charge. Look to her for guidance." He sat in thought for a moment, then said, "I want you to go on an errand to the squire this afternoon."

Mother looked up quickly and he went on, "In these days of difficult communication it is only friendly to let him know that I am going to the river. Belike he will have messages to send."

Mother smiled. "A good idea, Randall, a very good idea!"

71

Randy grinned. Pretty clever of Father! "You didn't used to be so thoughtful of the squire," he said.

"Times have changed."

"How about the haying? If I go to the squire's I'll have no time to help."

"Cynthia is going to have a lesson in hay making. She will have to help while I am gone, so she might as well practice."

Help in the field! Cynthia hated the thought. She would get sunburned, maybe even freckled. It was hot, dirty work.

"You must wear a deep bonnet which will keep the sun off your face," Mother said, as if reading her thoughts. "And gloves."

"Now Mary," Father protested, "the child can't work with blinders on."

"It is the only way she can go into the field," Mother said firmly. "Otherwise, I will help with the haying."

"I wish neither of you had to." Father shoved his plate aside. "Bring me writing material, daughter. I will write a message to the squire."

As Randy went through the woods with his note, he had an impulse to call on the old man. He hesitated, recalling the other's emphatic words, "Stay away from here tomorrow, lad. This food will do me. My ankle is mending. Less you hang around, less chance of my hidey-hole being discovered by those who would harm me. I have things to do, boy, important things. That's why I must stay alive."

It was that last sentence which decided Randy. Suppose the ankle wasn't mending, or that wound on his head. With no more hesitation he turned toward the quarry.

He was almost there before he thought to slow down and scout around a bit. He slipped into a thick growth of bushes and set himself to listen. His father had told him, "Use your ears, son. They'll tell you things before your eyes can. There are always noises going on in the woods. When they stop, you stop too, and see what made them stop."

Randy listened. Far away a cow mooed. That didn't prove anything. Nearer, birds twittered contentedly. Everything must be all right. He started to rise, then sank back as the peace of the forest was shattered by a shriek of terror. There was a crashing in the underbrush. The shrieking came closer. "Injuns! Injuns!"

Peter Estry's voice! And here came Peter dashing toward him, casting terrified glances over his shoulder.

Randy jumped up. "Where are they?"

Peter didn't slow his pace, so Randy ran too. "He grabbed for me," gasped the boy. "He'd have scalped me—"

"Was there only one?"

Peter wasted no more breath in talking. Though Randy pressed him with questions he said no more —only ran. Since he was running toward the squire's, Randy went along. He wondered if Peter had really seen an Indian. A worrisome thought came to him. Maybe Peter had peeped into the fissure and seen the old man. "Where was the Indian?" he asked.

When Peter didn't reply, Randy seized his arm and halted him. "You'll not go until you answer me," he declared. "Where was he?"

Peter tried to squirm out of Randy's grasp. "We'll both be scalped."

Randy tightened his grip. "Where was he?"

"By the stepping stones in the creek. He was beside me before I knew he was near."

Randy drew a breath of relief. That was well away from the quarry. "What did he say?" he asked. "What did he do?"

"He said naught I could understand. But his eyes—his eyes—" He glanced back terrified anew. "Let me go. He can come on us silent as a shadow."

Randy released him. "Come tell the squire of your Indian."

They found the squire sitting in a great carved chair smoking his pipe. Dencie was near, working at an embroidery frame.

Randy stayed back and let Peter deliver his news first.

"Indians?" the squire exclaimed, surprised.

Dencie squealed, "We'll all be murdered."

"Nonsense!" snapped her father. "Since when have you been afraid of Indians? You were always amused at them and loved to buy their gewgaws."

"That was long ago and they were friendly."

"These are no doubt friendly, too, perhaps messengers from the British. Randy, you are older than Peter and should have more sense, though your escapade at school would not prove it. What can you tell of these Indians?"

"Not much, sir. Peter came running through the woods yelling about them. As I was bringing you a message, we came on together."

"A message? Give it here, boy."

Randy handed him the paper and stood looking out the window so he wouldn't have to look at Dencie whom he detested. He couldn't shut out her shrill, unpleasant voice. "Peter, look at your boots! Go and clean them this instant."

Randy peeked at his own boots. They were dusty. He was half-minded to follow Peter out of the room, then thought better of it. Let her try and send him out—just let her!

The squire made gratified murmurs as he read the note. "So thoughtful of your father! I will take advantage of his offer and have messages ready. As he says, it is essential to keep headquarters informed. 'A link!' Ah, that is well put! He calls me

76

an important link in a chain. And, of course, I am in my small way." His pleased smirk made Randy feel positively ill.

On the stoop outside, Peter was busy rubbing his boots with some leaves. Randy saw him stiffen and stare into the woods, then leap up and bolt into the house. "Injuns!" he shouted. "They're coming!"

CHAPTER 8

"Injuns!" Peter's voice quavered with terror. "Injuns! We'll all be scalped."

"Hush your noise," the squire ordered. "All I can see is one unarmed Indian coming up the path. Think you he would come thus openly if he were bent on mischief?"

Peter ceased his outcry, but still shook as with ague.

Maybe it wasn't to be wondered at, thought Randy, considering that Peter's father and two big brothers had been killed in an Indian raid in the Mohawk Valley the year before.

The tall, scantily clad Indian stalked onto the stoop and into the room without a by-your-leave. He stood still for a moment, his piercing glance resting in turn on each person present. Then he advanced to the squire.

"Welcome!" the squire said. "You come as a messenger?"

The Indian nodded.

"Will you have something to eat?"

The Indian shook his head. "Grunting Bear," he said in a deep voice, placing his hand on his

78

chest. He pointed a finger at the squire. "You chief here." It was a statement rather than a question.

"Why, yes," the squire answered. "You might call me that. Yes, that fits right well, I must say." He beamed up at the bronze face which changed expression not at all. "Now about those dispatches, where are they?"

Grunting Bear stared at him in silence.

"The papers? In there, belike?" The squire gestured toward a leather pouch at the Indian's waist.

Grunting Bear looked at the other man for a moment, then opened the pouch and took out a piece of brown, withered meat and offered it to him.

The squire motioned the jerky away in great distaste. "No. Not that. Put it away before it scents the room. The message—give me the message."

Grunting Bear took his time replacing the meat in his pouch. Then he straightened up and his voice boomed forth sonorously, "The great chief from the North bids me tell you by what way the food offering should be sent to him."

"'The great chief from the North.' Why, that must be General Burgoyne himself. He must indeed be in dire plight when he tends personally to such details."

"There is great hunger among the redcoats," said the Indian.

"We must see that our donation reaches him safely and soon. How said he they were to come?"

Grunting Bear did not reply at once, but looked from one of the children to another. He indicated all three with a wave of his hand. "The young chatter like squirrels. The message is for your ear alone."

"Certainly. I should have thought of that. Dencie, Peter, Randy—get out of here at once."

Randy hated to leave. "What of the messages for Father? He leaves before daylight tomorrow."

"I will get them to him this evening. Run along now. And Dencie, see that I am not disturbed while I confer with this messenger."

Randy was first out the door, not wanting words with either Peter or Dencie. As he went down the path he heard her directing Peter to weed the herb garden. He pitied anyone, even Peter, who was at Dencie's beck and call.

One good thing though, if Peter were busy there he couldn't snoop after him. Now would be the time to see the old man. He'd tell him about the Indian. It would hearten him to know the British were hungry. If only he could have heard how the supplies were to be sent out, the old man might have sent word and had them destroyed. He was so deep in thought that he forgot to stop and listen.

He was at the entrance to the fissure when a voice snarled, "Get away from here quick. I told you not to come."

For an instant Randy was too startled to speak, then he stammered, "I wanted to be sure—"

"Git away!"

"But there's an Indian—"

"Git!"

Randy "got." He hurried without stopping until he was almost home. Then he slowed down and gave way to hurt and anger. Fine thing talking that way to him after all he'd done! He had a notion never to go near the old man again. But mingled with his anger was a feeling of guilt. Suppose he had brought harm to the old man by going there. Or worse yet, harm to the cause they both loved. He plodded home filled with disgust at himself.

He went at once to the hay meadow to report to his father. It was proof of how low he felt that he didn't jeer at Cynthia, who was wearing a bonnet so large he couldn't see her face.

She pushed it back at first mention of the Indian and listened excitedly, though with none of the foolish outcry Dencie had made.

Father questioned Randy closely concerning the appearance of the Indian. He laughed heartily when Randy told of Grunting Bear offering jerky to the squire. He didn't seem surprised that Burgoyne's army was hungry. "The rebels are at them every time they try to forage," he said.

Randy asked, "Who told you this, Father? Did we have visitors while I was gone?"

"There were men at the smithy talking."

"At the smithy?"

"Maje had a loose shoe. Well, now that you are back, you may take the scythe and I will go to other duties. The chairs must be wrapped for hauling."

As he walked briskly to the house, Randy stared after him. "When did he take Maje to the smithy? I hadn't heard of it."

"What difference?" snapped Cynthia. "All that matters is when will night come so I can leave this horrid job? My hands are blistered."

"They'll toughen up," Randy said, unfeelingly.

Father was in fine spirits that evening. "You'd think he was glad to get away," Randy said to Cynthia as they did the household chores while Mother helped pack.

"Who wouldn't be glad to get free of that haying?" Cynthia examined her reddened palms tenderly. "I'd sing for joy if I could get out of it."

"You think about yourself too much. If you could put your mind—" The brotherly lecture was cut short by the appearance of the squire.

"Thought I'd better bring my dispatches," he

said. "They're so important that I wanted to instruct you myself on what to do with them."

"I am glad you did," Father approved. "I want to be sure they get into the right hands."

"Your boy told you, of course, of the Indian messenger?"

Father nodded.

"It was well he came when he did or I would have sent the supplies by the wrong trail, belike to have them land in enemy hands."

"It was indeed fortunate that he came," Father agreed. "How are they to go? Or perhaps I should not have asked," he added as the squire hesitated.

"It is not that I do not trust you implicitly, my friend, but the fewer who know, the less chance of some word being let slip."

Randy was disappointed. He had hoped to hear something to tell the old man.

Father nodded hearty approval. "I'm better not knowing. If aught goes wrong, no blame can attach to me."

"Nothing will go wrong," Squire Telford declared. "It is a smart plan, yet simple. It will fool the rebels, never fear. Now as to this dispatch." He handed Father a folded paper, heavily sealed. "Have you some safe place in which to carry it?"

"Yes, I will put it in—"

"Hold!" The squire glanced at Randy. "As my messenger so aptly said, 'The young chatter like squirrels.' It might be well not to make public your hiding place."

Randy flushed angrily and looked at his father, who stowed the paper in his pouch and said, "Good advice! Loose talk can cause much trouble."

Squire Telford soon took his leave and Father hustled the family to bed. "We'll all have a hard day tomorrow," he said. "So let's get all the rest we can."

"Will you waken us to say goodbye when you go?" Cynthia asked.

"No. I want no one up." He kissed the girls and gave Randy a pat on the shoulder. "My lieutenant!" he said. "I'm depending on you."

"Aye, aye, captain!" Randy saluted smartly. "I won't fail you." He mounted the stairs wishing that it were true Father was a captain. Wishing he, too, could go on a secret mission.

Dawn was showing faintly when Cynthia woke him. "Father's going," she whispered. "I looked out the window. Oh, I'd like to go down and kiss him goodbye!"

"He told us not to." Randy crept out of bed and watched as the wagon rolled away. Mother stood waving until it was out of sight, then walked slowly to the house.

"She looks so sad and lonely." Cynthia sniffed, and rubbed her eyes on her sleeve.

"Of course, she's lonesome." Randy spoke

sharply. He hated sniffles. "But Father will be back in two or three days." He laughed. "Time will fly in the hayfield."

He went back to bed wondering what his father's real purpose was in making the trip. Not to sell chairs he was sure. He wondered into whose hands the squire's messages would fall. He wished that his father would let him share his work. Well, at least there was the old man. That was his secret.

They did not make hay the next morning because the supplies had to be taken to the tavern. "Father wants you to take an extra shoat," Mother said. "The one you call 'Greedy.'"

"He's the biggest one," protested Randy.

"No arguing. We will do as Father wishes. He is glad to do it for the cause."

"Such a cause!"

"You promised you would be careful of your speech," Mother interrupted. "Practice it at home and you will have less trouble abroad."

Randy flushed. "I mean to, Mother, but words come bursting out."

His mother put her hand on his shoulder. "Every time they start bursting out remember that your brave father's life depends on your silence. Then it will be easier to choke them back."

"How will Randy get two shoats, two lambs and some other things to the tavern?" Cynthia asked.

"You'll have to help me," Randy said.

"Me go to the tavern? I can't do that."

"Of course you can't," Mother agreed. "But you can go to the edge of the woods. Randy can take some of the things to the tavern while you keep the rest. It will not be too far for you to make a second trip from the woods to the tavern, will it, son?"

"No, that will be easy. We'll get everything there in good shape, I promise you, Mother."

"Let me go," begged Polly. She seized her mother's hand. "Please, please, Mother. Maybe I'll see my little friend."

"What friend?" asked Randy.

"The little girl. The one that comes and looks at me through the fence."

"Oh, the make-believe one," laughed Randy.

"She is *not* make believe. She has pretty black curls and wears a red dress."

"Polly, Polly, you must not pretend so much," her mother chided. "I think I'll let you go with Cynthia. Maybe if you got out more you wouldn't live in such a dream world. Pick some berries, Cynthia. They would taste right good for supper."

"I'll take some lunch," Cynthia said, "and we'll eat on the way."

They started out with Randy driving the shoats and carrying the meat. Cynthia brought the lambs and dried apples. Polly chased butterflies, picked flowers and looked for her "friend." She called, "Little girl, little girl, where are you?"

The older children's amusement was tinged with pity as they realized how lonesome their little sister was.

They had their hands full with the animals. Randy's shoats were reluctant to travel and had to be prodded along. The lambs were as eager as Polly to run about. They were constantly entangling the ropes with which Cynthia led them, and made her step nimbly to keep from getting tripped.

"If I didn't have this sack of apples, I could lead them better," she sighed.

"Think how dear General Burgoyne will love the apple pies," Randy said. He gave Greedy a hard whack with his stick. "Get along there! What do you think I fattened you up for? Why, for the British army, of course."

Cynthia heaved a sigh of relief when they reached the edge of the woods. "There, now all Polly and I have to do is wait for you to come back." She tied the lambs to a bush and started looking for berries while Randy went to the tavern with the shoats.

Cynthia soon found a patch of luscious berries and settled down to pick. "We'll try and fill the bucket," she said. "Then Mother can make some preserves."

Polly nodded, her mouth too full of berries for talking.

Randy was back before they had the bucket half full. He came high-stepping along, his eyes shining, a grin on his face.

Cynthia stopped picking to stare at him. "What makes you look so happy?"

"We have a flag, Sis. Think of it. A flag."

"Who has?"

"The patriots, that's who. A flag of their own. Congress says so. It's red and white and blue. I heard a man tell what it looks like. I'll draw one when we get home."

The glow faded from his face, replaced by fierce anger. "The man laughed and called it 'a rebel rag,' and the others laughed. I almost choked keeping back words. Oh, well, we've got a flag. Some day they won't dare laugh at it." He untied the lambs, snatched up the apples, and hurried off, still treading on air.

Cynthia went back to her picking. A flag! That did make the new country seem more real. George Washington would soon be crowned king. She drifted off into pleasant daydreams.

She was recalled to the present by a tremendous shouting from the direction of the tavern. Startled, she sprang up and called Polly. There was no answer. She looked around. Polly was not to be seen.

CHAPTER 9

"Polly, Polly," Cynthia's voice rose in a terrified scream. The noise at the distant tavern increased but she no longer heard it. She ran wildly to and fro, calling, calling. At last she made herself stop and think more quietly. What would make Polly stray? Any of a dozen things—a bright butterfly, a bird, a chipmunk—most of all, her little friend. Suppose she had decided to look for her friend, where would she go? Not towards the tavern, and not towards home.

There was a little hill close by. She hurried to it, calling as she ran. There was little to see from its summit except trees and bushes and a grassy glade at one side.

"Polly," she called. "Polly, where are you?" From a bush across the glade a slight movement caught her eye. She sped down the slope and around the bush. There was Polly, laying sticks in a pattern on the ground.

Relief made Cynthia's voice sharp. "Polly, why didn't you answer? You must have heard me."

"I was too busy building a house for my friend. See, there she is. Hasn't she pretty curls!"

Cynthia looked up and gasped. Coming out of the bushes was a child about Polly's age. She had black curls and a red dress, faded but clean. She was carrying a load of sticks and smiling. The smile faded as she saw Cynthia. She dropped the sticks and turned away.

Polly ran and seized her hand. "Don't be afraid. It's my sister. She won't hurt you."

So Polly's "friend" was real after all! Cynthia recovered from her surprise enough to ask, "Who are you?"

Before the child could speak, there came a worried shout, "Lottie, Lottie!"

"It's Peter," the little girl said. "He'll take me home."

"Are you Peter's sister?" Cynthia asked.

The child nodded.

Cynthia, remembering her recent terror, called, "Peter, she's here behind the hill."

"He'll take me away," Lottie said. "We can't make our house."

"Don't let him, Cynthia," Polly begged. "We want to play."

Peter came charging around the hill, breathless and angry. He seized Lottie as if to shake her, then his expression softened. "How could you scare me so, Lottie? Why didn't you stay at home like I told you?"

"Is your mother at home?" Cynthia asked.

"No, she has to work."

"Then you—"

"I have to work, too."

Spying for the squire, Cynthia thought, but she didn't say so.

Lottie shrugged loose from her brother. "Let's make the house," she said to Polly. At once the two were absorbed in their play and paid no attention to their elders.

"Aren't they adorable!" Cynthia exclaimed, feeling for the first time a sense of companionship with Peter. "Your sister is so pretty! She's sweet and clean, too. Her hair shines like silk."

Peter's eyes glowed. "They look nice together, one so light, one so dark. I wish—"

Cynthia didn't find out what he wished. There came a sound of galloping horses on the road. Men were shouting. Guns were fired.

"Oh, what is it?" she gasped. "Randy's at the tavern." She seized Polly and ran. Peter followed with Lottie.

The noise increased as they neared the road. They could see men riding up and down, firing guns and shouting. They stopped well within the shelter of the trees and tried to figure out what was going on.

"They're firing in the air," Peter said.

"They don't sound angry," Cynthia added, "just

excited. Can you understand what they are yelling?"

"No, but they sound glad about something."

They were so absorbed in watching that Randy was beside them before they saw him. "Randy, you frightened me!" Cynthia exclaimed. "What's happening? Why are they shouting?"

"Lot of riffraff." Ignoring Peter, Randy seized Polly's hand. "We're going home right now."

"But the strawberries," protested Cynthia. "And our lunch!"

"We'll eat it at home." He started through the trees, not heeding Polly's protest.

What made him act like this, Cynthia wondered. Maybe because Peter was there. She picked up the strawberry pail and parcel of food. On an impulse she handed the food to Lottie. "You and Peter can have lunch here," she said. "And some day you come over to play with Polly."

"Did you have to be so unkind, Randy?" she scolded when she had caught up with him. "Why couldn't we have had our lunch, and even asked Peter and his sister? And Mother wanted us to get some strawberries."

Randy turned a face toward her so full of pain, so hopeless and sad, that she gasped, "Randy, what's the matter?"

"Fort Ticonderoga has fallen."

"You mean the British—"

"Took it with hardly a shot fired. I couldn't tell you before Peter and have him gloat."

"Is that what the shouting is about?"

"Yes. The news just came and the Tories went wild. They say the war is as good as over. Maybe they're right."

"No, Randy, no!" Cynthia surprised both herself and Randy by her earnestness. "The patriots will never give up. Remember what the man said, 'Liberty or death.'"

Randy's expression lightened a little. "Sis, do you believe that?"

"Yes I do. George Washington will never give up. Neither will Father. Never, never, never."

"And neither will I," declared Randy.

Polly pulled at his hand. "Come on home. I want to tell Mother how unkind you were, not letting me play with my friend."

"You tell Mother the news," Randy said when they reached home. "I can't bear to see her face when she hears it." He took the scythe and went down to the meadow.

But no sooner had Cynthia told her story than her mother ran out to the meadow to get the news first hand.

"A man brought the report that the British took the fort three days ago," Randy told her. "The men at the tavern began yelling and firing their guns. I came away."

Mother clenched her hands. Her face was pale. Randy looked at her in alarm. "Don't take it so hard, Mother," he said. "This isn't the end."

She managed a smile. "No, of course it's not." She stood silent for a moment. "The end will be different, very different. And pray God it will come soon!" She turned and walked swiftly to the house.

When Randy went in at noon, his mother said, "I want you to go to the tavern. There might be later news. Stay out of trouble, but get news."

Randy, about to remind her of the haying, thought better of it. There might be more news. The first report might even be wrong. He hurried away, hope rising at every step.

"You and I will put up hay," Mother told Cynthia. Presently, protected by sunbonnets, neckerchiefs and gloves, with Polly and Primrose trailing behind, they went to the meadow.

At any other time Mother's efforts to use the scythe would have brought gales of laughter. Today, there was no laughter in mother or daughter.

Trying to think of something to make her mother smile, Cynthia remembered the flag. "Mother," she exclaimed, "we have a flag."

Her mother looked up bewildered. "A flag?"

"Randy heard the man at the tavern describe it. It's red and white and blue with stripes and stars."

"A flag of our own!" Mother said. "Red, white

and blue—same colors as the mother country. Stars in it you say? That makes it different. Sounds right pretty. I'd like to see one."

Randy said he could draw one from the description the man gave."

A smile touched Mother's lips. "A flag of our own! It heartens me to think of it. Makes our cause seem more real. Helps me forget the news you brought this morning. God speed the day when it will float over a free people!" She stood for a moment, turning the thought over in her mind. "Well, to work, daughter. This is what you and I can do while your father risks his life."

"Risks his life?" gasped Cynthia. "How—"

"Some things are better not discussed." Mother set her lips firmly and began wielding the scythe with more energy than skill.

Randy was back by supper time. There was no further news. The celebration was getting wilder by the hour. Squire Telford was trying to calm things down with little success.

"He was looking for Master Bundy," Randy said. "He thought perhaps they'd listen to him as he's such a good speech maker. The squire couldn't find him. He was in a rare temper." Randy grinned at the memory of the squire's anger.

"Master Bundy is supposed to be at home," Mother said, surprised.

"Yes, he had to hoe his corn. That's why we're having a vacation," Cynthia said.

Randy nodded. "That's what the squire thought. He called Peter a 'stupid dolt' when he couldn't find Master Bundy, and sent me to look. He wasn't in the field so I asked the woman who cooks for him. She said he had gone to Albany for school supplies."

"What supplies?" Cynthia asked, surprised. "We have copy books and slates and paper."

"The squire asked the same thing," Randy said, grinning again. "I told him Master Bundy sent me out to get birch bark to do sums on."

"Why, Randy, you know he did that because he said you were careless with the paper, not because there was a shortage."

"I know. I didn't tell the squire, though. Master Bundy has a right to go away without telling the squire. Who does he think he is? A king?"

His mother looked alarmed. "You must be careful what you say to the squire. Don't let your dislike of him make you imprudent."

"I won't. Why, you should have seen me helping him look for Master Bundy. I looked everywhere. He said it wasn't my fault I couldn't find him. I thought that was right nice."

Mother couldn't help smiling at his tone. But there was little smiling in the Stewart household that night. At bedtime, Mother had them repeat the twenty-third psalm. This had been their nightly custom when Father was away before. It made the children realize how worried their mother was.

"Did you fix food for the old man?" Randy asked Cynthia when they had gone upstairs.

"Yes. I put in some little cakes, too, because he'll feel so bad about the news."

"I'm not going to tell him. He'll feel so helpless shut up there. And yet, maybe he should know. He might need to send a message. Oh, I don't know what to do!"

He climbed down the oak tree in this uncertain mood and came back in a worse one. "He's gone," he reported.

"Gone?" gasped Cynthia. "Do you think—"

"I don't know what to think. I couldn't see, of course, but I felt around. The blanket is gone, and the jug. I'm going back in the morning."

"Oh, don't, Randy. Whoever took him may be watching. You mustn't go near the place with the Tories feeling so high and mighty."

"Perhaps you're right," Randy agreed.

It was hard next day to stick by that sensible decision. Maybe the old man was lying hurt somewhere. The thought was more than Randy could stand. "I've got to do something," he said.

"Wait until it's dark," Cynthia begged.

"I don't think I can wait that long." But Randy put off going for a while, knowing Cynthia was right.

The haying dragged endlessly. At noon, Cynthia went to the house to help her mother with the mid-day meal. Randy, his mind on the old man, swung his scythe with listless strokes. When a shadow fell on his path, he looked up startled to see Grunting Bear at his shoulder. He had one wild moment of panic before the Indian spoke.

"White Hair is safe," he said, and strode away.

CHAPTER 10

"White Hair is safe." That must mean the old man. How would the Indian know? "Grunting Bear," Randy called, running after him. "Where is he? Where is the old man?"

Grunting Bear did not turn nor alter his stride. He merely made a fierce backward motion with his arm which said as plainly as words, "Go back!"

Randy stopped and watched until the tall figure had disappeared into the woods. He knew it was useless to follow.

Back at work, the puzzling thought returned to him. How did Grunting Bear know about the old man? He was a messenger of the British. *Or was he?* Could Grunting Bear have tricked the squire? He had no dispatches. If that were so, those supplies would fall into the hands of the patriots. Randy chuckled at the thought.

Still, it wouldn't make much difference now. The British could get plenty of supplies at Fort Ti. Even that thought didn't make him feel the world had come to an end as it had the day before. The old man was safe. That much was right. Maybe other things would be right, too.

"White Hair is safe. White Hair is safe." The swish of the scythe made a cheery refrain. Presently Randy added another line, "One battle doesn't win a war." That was what the squire had said about Washington's victory at Trenton. Well, it could work both ways. "White Hair is safe. One battle doesn't win a war." Each time he repeated the refrain, he felt better. When the dinner bell rang he bounded to the house as if on seven league boots.

"What's for dinner?" he shouted. "I'm hungry."

His mother and sister looked at him astonished. It was plain they didn't share his high spirits. "Make yourself tidy and you'll find out," Mother said.

"I can have old Cynthia smiling in no time," he thought as he went out on the porch to wash. When she came out on her way to the buttery, he told her the message he had from Grunting Bear.

"Oh!" she cried. "That's wonderful! But—" she paused uncertainly. "Randy, how can you trust that Indian? He's a friend of the British. Maybe they've taken the old man prisoner. Maybe he'll be shot as a spy."

"Why would Grunting Bear come and tell me unless he was the old man's friend?"

Cynthia thought that over for a moment and cheered up. "That's right. Wasn't it thoughtful of the old man—"

"What old man are you talking about? I thought

you were getting the milk for dinner." There was Mother, standing right behind them!

Cynthia, too flustered for words, fled to the buttery. Randy's voice stopped her. "We might as well tell Mother all about it now."

"I'd like to," stammered Cynthia. "I hated having a secret from her."

"What is this secret?" Mother asked.

"We found an old man lying in the quarry. His head was cut and his ankle was sprained," Randy explained.

"We wanted to bring him here but he wouldn't come," Cynthia added.

"So we fixed his wounds and hid him in a cave— that place Father told us to stay out of because of falling rock. That night I took him food."

"Was that the night your father went out to the barn?"

"Yes. Cynthia was watching for me. That's why she saw him. I didn't go the next night. He told me not to. Last night when I went, he was gone. We felt awful."

"He was the same old man that told Randy the verse that got him into trouble," Cynthia said. "We were afraid—"

"Afraid it would get Father into trouble with the squire. That's why we were so secretive about it. All the morning we felt worse and worse. I knew

I'd have to do something soon. Then the Indian came and said the old man was safe. 'White Hair is safe,' he said. That's all he would tell me."

"There's safety in not knowing things sometimes," Mother said. "I shall be interested to see what happens when your father hears this story."

Randy looked at his mother in alarm. "Must you you tell him? It's all over. He'll never trust me again."

"Should he? Mother looked at her son's downcast face and her voice softened. "You did it to be kind. Any decent person would do the same."

Randy was silent for a moment, then blurted, "That wasn't the only reason. The old man believes what we do. I'd help him no matter how dangerous."

"Yes," Mother said soberly. "When occasion arises we must not think of our personal safety. Opportunities must be seized."

"You mean that, Mother?" Randy's eyes were shining. "Can I go out and—"

"No, no, Randy! Our part is to conduct ourselves in such a way that no suspicion falls on your father. For then his usefulness would end. So would his life. This is our whole duty. Helping the old man was a natural act of kindness and could be decried by no one. Airing your motives for doing it could be dangerous. See what a careful path you must tread?"

"Yes, I see. It's a hard thing—doing nothing and covering your real feelings."

"Hard but necessary. Now, Cynthia, get the milk. You hay makers must eat and get back to work."

Little was said during dinner until Polly began chattering about her friend Lottie.

"So now you've named her." Mother roused from serious thoughts to smile at her daughter.

"I didn't name her, did I, Cynthia?" Polly protested. "Her brother called her Lottie."

"She's Peter's sister," Cynthia explained. "We saw her yesterday. I forgot to tell you because I was so excited about the news."

"So that's the Estry child—Polly's friend. Poor lonesome tot, with her mother working at the tavern and Peter at the squire's."

"Why don't they stay at home and take care of her?" Cynthia demanded. "You wouldn't leave Polly that way."

"I don't have to, thank God. Your father provides for us. Lottie's father is dead, so her mother does hard, disagreeable work to keep her children clothed and fed. She is to be admired."

"Peter snoops for the squire because he likes to snoop," Randy declared.

"That may be, but it is also true that the squire owns the house—hardly more than a hut—where the

Estrys live. Peter pays the rent by working for the squire."

"I didn't know that," Randy said. "I still don't like his snooping. He'd better stay away from here."

"Do you think I can trust you to go to the tavern again today?" Mother asked. "There'll be many a short temper due to yesterday's carousing. It will be necessary to guard your tongue with extra care."

"I'll be careful," Randy promised. "I'd do anything to keep Father safe."

"I know you would, son. Remember, though, that it is doing nothing that will accomplish most."

Randy's trip to the tavern did not cheer them. The British had fallen upon fleeing patriots and inflicted heavy loss, though not on the main body of "rebels." They had got clean away. Tories along the river were warned to watch for them. They'd be falling back in numbers, no doubt.

Randy kept his eyes open as he went through the woods. He'd like nothing better than to help a wounded patriot.

The squire was busy supervising the packing and loading of supplies. Randy heard men arguing with him. Why send them, they asked. The British would have all the food they needed from the fort. Others argued that with hungry rebels roaming about, the supplies were in danger of being stolen.

The squire stood firm. The British would need supplies as they came south. There was no danger of their being stolen the way he was going to send them. He made quite a mystery of the route. No one was to know it except himself and the teamsters.

And Grunting Bear, thought Randy, wondering anew if it could be that the Indian was tricking Squire Telford. He hoped so.

"The celebration is over," he reported at home. "Hardly anyone is at the tavern today." He told what he had heard about the retreating army. "The squire said for you not to worry because patrols would see that 'the scoundrels' didn't bother us. The words are his, not mine," he added in such a disgusted tone that his mother laughed.

"No word of Master Bundy, I suppose," she asked.

"No. The squire didn't mention him and I didn't see him in the field."

That night Randy drew a picture of the new flag with its red and white stripes and circle of stars. He showed it to his mother. "Right pretty, isn't it?" He tried not to sound as choked up as he felt.

She nodded, studying it intently. "The same colors as the flag under which your ancestors have fought for many years, but how different it looks with the stars! I like them. I like this flag. It will be a proud day when it waves over our house."

She studied it a bit longer, then handed it back to Randy. "Now it's nothing to have in the house for decoration," she said, and resumed her knitting.

"I suppose not." Randy stuffed it in his pocket. Upstairs he and Cynthia looked at it again.

"I think I can make one out of cloth," Cynthia said. "I have some red and blue scraps in my bag."

"Could you, Sis? That would be wonderful. We'll put it here on the wall where we can look at it every day."

"I don't think we should have it on the wall," Cynthia said. "We'd better hide it."

"We'll see when we get it done. Can you get it made by tomorrow?"

"Goodness, no! It will take days and days. I'll only be able to work at it in odd minutes."

"You'll never have any odder minutes than now, so let's get started."

"Now?" Cynthia exclaimed in surprise. "I haven't any star pattern."

"I'll make you one. Get some cloth."

Cynthia rummaged in her piece bag and found red, white and blue scraps. Randy made a star pattern and cut out pieces while she sewed. They worked silently so that they wouldn't wake Polly or their mother. Finally Randy called a reluctant halt. "If we're going to make hay tomorrow, we'll have to get some sleep," he said. They put all evidence of their work away in Cynthia's bag.

Father was home when they came downstairs

next morning. "Fine trip!" he said. "Made connection with the boat captain without delay."

"You heard the news, Father?" Randy asked.

"About Fort Ti? Yes. A serious setback no one can deny. But," he squared his shoulders and smiled confidently, "only a temporary setback."

"Tell your father about the old man," Mother said.

Stammering a little under his father's grave look, Randy told the story. "You'd have done it, too," he finished. "You wouldn't leave an old man to die."

"Certainly not. You did right to help him. And I appreciate your reasons in not telling me about it. However, if another occasion arises, please tell me about it, son. It may be something which would influence my actions. I have to keep so many things from you because they are not my secrets, and because it is safer for us if you do not know. But it would be a great help to me if you would tell all the significant facts you see and hear."

"I'll report on anything I find out," Randy promised with such eagerness that his father added, "Don't go out of your way to collect information. Don't be a 'peeping Peter.' You are a simple Tory schoolboy, and do not make yourself conspicuous at any time or place, remember."

"I'll remember," Randy said in such a different tone that both his parents laughed.

"Oh, I have something to show you, Father,"

Randy said. He dashed upstairs and returned with the picture. "Here's our flag," he said. "I heard at the tavern that Congress had adopted it as our flag."

Father took the picture and studied it. "Saw one like it down the river. Fellow had a little one on his hat. Right pretty!" His tone conveyed much more than his words. Randy knew that his father was deeply moved.

"Yes, a fine flag to fight under," he said. "But deadly to have here now. You know that, son."

Randy nodded.

His father handed back the bit of paper. "Burn this and don't make another."

"Burn it?" Randy held the picture close and looked at his father in mute protest.

"Burn it now."

Randy stalked across the room and threw the paper into the fire.

"Time to get to work." Father rose from the table.

That night when they had gone upstairs and Polly was asleep, Randy whispered, "Get out your pieces and get to work."

"Why, Randy Stewart, Father told us not to make another."

"He told me, not you."

"You know what he meant, though."

Randy faced his sister. In the flickering candle-light, his expression was troubled. "Sis, I've thought

111

about it all day. We have to have a flag. It will give us courage. It will make us feel we really have a country. When things go wrong, we can take it out and look at it."

"You take it out and Father would make you burn it as he did the pattern."

"We won't take it downstairs. We'll hide it up here and look at it when we need to renew our courage."

"It won't help Father and Mother."

"It will strengthen us and we can give courage to them. I've got to have that flag, Sis." Randy looked so forlorn Cynthia couldn't help but pity him.

He took hold of her arm. "Think of the day when the war is won," he whispered. "We could bring it out. Father and Mother would be so happy to see it."

Against her judgment, Cynthia tiptoed to the chest of drawers and got out her piece bag. Soon she was busy putting neat little stitches in the flag.

It didn't take long to finish it. The next thing was to find a hiding place.

"In my commode drawer, down beneath the clothes will be a good place," Cynthia said. "Mother never looks there."

"What about Polly? She likes to snoop."

"I gave her the bottom drawer for her very own. She keeps her things there and plays games of packing and unpacking. She doesn't pay any attention to my drawer."

Every night they took the flag out and looked at it. Every night it became dearer to them. Gradually their feeling of guilt in its possession faded.

The rest of the haying went slowly. Father had to be away to help patrol the countryside against fleeing "rebels." Strangely enough he found none, though he brought back reports of having sighted them in the distance, even of having taken shots at them.

Then came the news that the supplies for the British had been stolen. Father took a couple of men to hunt for the thieves. They found no trace of them.

"Grunting Bear surely tricked the squire," Randy said to Cynthia. "I had a hard time not to laugh when the squire told it. The British are having other trouble, too. Burgoyne is bringing his troops by land instead of water. The patriots are chopping down trees in the way. They made Woods Creek overflow and stopped the lobsterbacks. Get out the flag, Sis. Maybe soon we won't have to hide it any more."

Cynthia went to get it. She came back empty-handed. "It's gone!" she said. "The flag's gone!"

CHAPTER 11

"Gone?" gasped Randy. "I don't believe it. Where could it go? You missed it in the dark. Take the candle and look again."

"It's not there," Cynthia repeated. "I always put it in the same place." But she took the candle and hunted again.

Randy helped her. They took everything out of the drawer and looked. They did the same for Polly's. They searched every part of the room. At last they had to give up.

"Mother found it and took it away without saying anything," Randy decided.

"Mother hasn't been up here," Cynthia said, trying to keep back the tears.

"How do you know? You raked hay all day. Well, it's gone. There's nothing we can do. If Father gets hold of it we'll hear soon enough."

As this failed to cheer her, he went on, "Father will be angry but I'll tell him it was my fault, not yours." He grinned. "Anyway we know Peter Estry wasn't up here snooping around, so Squire Telford won't get hold of it. Go to bed and forget it."

Easier said than done. Both of them lay awake

a long time dreading the morning and Father's accusing look.

They were more mystified than relieved when neither parent mentioned the flag.

Master Bundy came back and school was resumed. The weather was hot. The British were advancing down the Hudson. Liberty and a grand new nation seemed to have vanished with the flag.

School was progressing at a drowsy pace one day when the door burst open and in came Squire Telford followed by a couple of Tory militiamen armed with long rifles.

"That's him!" one of the men exclaimed, pointing at Master Bundy. "That's the spy we caught at Newhall last month. He got away before we could hang him."

"Master Bundy, I arrest you," shouted the squire. "In the name of—"

Crash! Master Bundy was through the window in one leap, and racing towards the woods.

The soldiers fired through the window, but missed. They dashed for the door. Someone had barred it. Randy, making fumbling attempts to open it, was shoved aside by the men. Before they could get outside, the schoolmaster had disappeared.

The whole school streamed out to follow the squire and his men in their pursuit. At the edge of the woods, Randy stopped them. "We might get

shot," he said. "Remember those long guns they had." To himself he thought, "Run fast, Master Bundy, run fast!" He didn't doubt that the schoolmaster was a spy. He remembered the look which had flashed for an instant in the schoolmaster's eyes when he had recited, "Give me liberty or give me death." Which would it be for Master Bundy, liberty or death?

People from the tavern came down the road, Peter's mother among them. "Master Bundy a spy?" she exclaimed. "And my boy going to school to him!"

As if "snooping Peter" needed lessons in spying! thought Randy in disgust.

The squire came back, puffing and tired. No, they hadn't caught him yet. But they would.

Someone asked how they had found out Bundy was a spy. "I'm convinced the fellow came up here to keep an eye on Burgoyne's advance," the squire said. "I'll admit the fellow fooled me for a while. Lately I've had my suspicions. Remember when he took that so-called trip to Albany, lad?" He turned to Randy, who nodded. "That's when I began a quiet investigation. When these men came today looking for an escaped spy, I took them to the school. They identified Bundy at once. Have no fear, good people, they'll get him. And when they do, we'll have a hanging, I promise you."

Randy felt he couldn't stand any more of such

talk. "Since we can't have school, is it all right to go home?" he asked.

"Yes, yes, go along home, you children. There'll be no school for a time. Your next teacher will be no spy. I'll guarantee that."

Once in the woods, Cynthia gave way to tears. "Think of it—Master Bundy hanged!"

"They'll have to catch him first. Save your crying till then. He got out of there fast, didn't he? Well, if he gets away he can thank me for giving him a little head start."

"What do you mean?"

"Who do you think barred the door? And who do you think kept it shut until the fellow shoved me away?"

Cynthia stopped crying to giggle. "You're so quick-witted and brave. I wouldn't have dared even if I'd thought of it."

Randy walked on in deep thought for a while. "There'll be danger for every patriot around here now," he said at last. Squire Telford will be snooping everywhere. Oh, I wish I knew where that flag went to. If they get hold of that, Father—"

"Randy!" squealed Cynthia. "Don't talk that way! You said you thought Mother had found the flag and destroyed it without saying anything so Father wouldn't whip you. That must be what happened, Randy. Nobody could have got up there and found it."

118

"I know they couldn't," Randy agreed. "This thing happening to Master Bundy upset me."

Mother looked up from her spinning in surprise as they entered the kitchen. "They came for Master Bundy," blurted Randy.

"Who?" she gasped, her face paling. "Who came?"

"Soldiers. They said he was a spy."

"Oh—oh—" Mother couldn't go on.

"They didn't get him. He jumped through the window and ran. For all I know, he's still running."

"Still running! Pray God he is! Now tell me all about it. It makes me fair dizzy to think of it."

They told her all. Randy's part won a smile from her and a pat on the shoulder.

"God will aid him," she said, as she got up to prepare the midday meal. "He will not let harm come to such a gallant man."

"I hope not," Randy said. "But remember Nathan Hale. He, too, was a brave man; yet he was hanged by the British."

"Don't!" Mother gasped, white to the lips. "Don't mention him. Don't think of him."

"She's worrying about Father, too," thought Randy, sorry he had spoken. To his mother he said, "You knew Master Bundy was a patriot, didn't you?"

She nodded. "Now don't ask me any more about him." After they had eaten, she sent Randy to the tavern. "Stay until night if you must, but get news," she said.

The day was hot. Cynthia put a blanket out under the oak tree for Polly to nap on. Polly had her doll in its cradle with her and was soon fast asleep.

Sometime later, Cynthia noticed that Polly was gone. She had probably wandered down to see the lambs. She loved them.

"Go and see," Mother said. "She might climb into the pigpen to see the little pigs. The old sow is vicious."

There was no sign of Polly in the barnyard. Cynthia looked into the woodlot and felt great relief at the sight of Polly watching a chipmunk.

"Polly," she called, "come here. You know you shouldn't climb the fence and go into the woods."

"My friend had to go home," Polly called, making no move. "I gave her my dolly."

"You what?"

"I gave her my dolly. Oh, Cynthia, she liked it so! She has never had a dolly."

"You gave away the nice dolly Father brought you from New York?"

"She didn't have any. I can play with yours."

"You can not." Cynthia climbed the fence and ran to Polly. "Show me where you played with the little girl."

Polly led the way to a shady nook framed by a clump of trees. "Here's our house," she said.

Cynthia looked around carefully. There was no sign of the missing doll. She jumped when a voice asked, "Looking for something?"

It was Peter Estry.

"Yes. Polly's doll. She says she gave it to your sister."

"Sure it's a doll you want, and not this?" Peter drew something from his pocket and unfolded it.

Cynthia gasped at the sight of the lost flag.

"Squire Telford will be glad to get this," taunted Peter.

Before Cynthia could get her breath, Polly cried, "That's my dolly blanket with stars. Give it to me." She snatched at it but Peter held it out of reach.

"Peter," Cynthia tried to make her voice firm, "if you don't give that to Polly, I'll tell Randy and he'll—"

"He'll have some explaining to do, and so will your father."

"Randy and my father haven't anything to do with it. I heard about the flag and I had some scraps so I made one to see what it would look like." She held out her hand. "If you'll give it to me—"

Peter made no move.

"Your little sister can have the doll."

"She's got it already."

Cynthia longed to snatch the flag but Peter was

121

stronger and could run faster. If only Randy were here! But he wasn't. She'd have to handle it herself. She stood in thought for a moment while Polly tried to get her "dolly blanket" and Peter held it out of her reach.

At last she said, "Peter, remember that doll cradle you wanted for your little sister? I'll give it to you if you give me the flag."

"You'd trick me."

Cynthia shook her head. "I give you my word. You know I don't lie like—" she stopped. "I don't lie," she repeated. "You know that."

Peter studied her in silence.

"With the doll and cradle, she'd be content to stay at home. You wouldn't have to worry about her." She could see that Peter was weakening. "It would help your mother. She must worry about Lottie."

For a little longer Peter stood silent, while Cynthia held her breath and tried to think of a prayer to say.

"Go and get it," he said, finally.

Cynthia, dizzy with relief, grabbed Polly's hand and started away. But no, she mustn't leave the flag in Peter's possession. "Come with me," she said.

"And have Randy wallop me? No thanks."

"I mean just to the fence. The cradle's under the oak tree. I'll hand it over the fence."

As he still hesitated, she said, "If you don't do that, I'll tell Randy and you'll get a beating you'll remember, I promise you that."

"And if we make the bargain?"

"He'll not bother you. I give you my word." She started away, calling over her shoulder, "So come or not as you please."

Brave words! But her heart didn't start beating until she heard him following.

Near the yard fence Peter stopped. Cynthia boosted Polly over, then picked up the cradle.

"Don't you give him my cradle," Polly cried. "Cynthia, don't."

"Please be still, Polly," Cynthia begged. "Be still a minute and sister will get you her doll."

"Will you, Cynthia?" Polly sat down on the ground. "Hurry!"

Cynthia handed the cradle across the fence and reached for the flag. Peter jerked the cradle, but she was prepared for such a trick and held on tightly. "I'll let go when you give me the flag," she said. "If you try any tricks, I'll yell."

He chucked the flag into her hand, took the cradle and ran. Cynthia clutched her treasure to her and flopped down on the grass crying.

Polly hurried to her. "Did he hurt you?" she asked. "Get up, Cynthia, get up and get me your dolly."

Cynthia folded the flag and put it in her pocket.

As she started for the house, she wondered what she should tell Mother about the cradle. But Mother was so absorbed in her own thoughts that she didn't notice her daughters.

Randy came home at supper time with no news, and feeling sad. When he went to the barn, Cynthia followed. "Look, Randy," she said, and pulled the flag from her pocket.

Randy stared in surprise, then gave a whoop of joy, and took it into his hands. "I'm glad to see it again. Where did you find it?"

"Polly was using it for a doll blanket and Peter Estry got it."

Alarm chased the joy from Randy's face. "Peter Estry? How did he happen to give it to you?"

She told him of the bargain she had been forced to make. Randy groaned. "He'll tell the squire—unless I threaten him. That's what I'll do."

"I promised you wouldn't."

"We can't let him get us into trouble, and Father, too."

"I promised. We'll burn this and deny we ever had it. It will be Peter's word against ours."

"We'll not burn it. This time I'll hide it where Polly can't get hold of it."

"That's silly. They'll search."

"They'll not find it where I put it. It will be guarded night and day."

"Don't talk foolish. You can't guard it all the time."

Randy laughed. "I won't have to. Something else will. Come, I'll show you." He climbed to the hayloft. Cynthia, still protesting, followed.

Along one side of the floor were open places where hay could be pitched into mangers below. Randy climbed through one of them. Cynthia, about to follow, drew back. "That's Snorter's," she exclaimed.

"He's out in front."

"He can come in, silly."

Snorter's stall opened directly onto his outdoor enclosure. There were bars which could shut him in or out. Father, the only one who ever tended the bull, had opened the bars before he went away, so that Snorter could have the freedom of the little paddock.

"He's drowsy now. I'll shut him out," Randy said, and lowered himself to the manger. He slid the bars into place, then walked to the back of the stall. Cynthia climbed cautiously down.

Randy pounded the boards at the back. "What do you think this is?"

"The back of the barn, of course."

"The back of the barn is made of logs."

"Well—" Cynthia hesitated, "maybe Father put boards there for extra warmth."

"No. Snorter's stall is two feet shorter than the other stalls. I found that out one day when Father made me clean it. He said the less room Snorter had, the easier it was to handle him."

"What does that have to do with hiding the flag?"

"I'll show you." Randy reached up and removed a board.

"There's a nice little hidey-hole that no one knows about except Father, and he'd never think about it."

"How did you know the board was loose?" Cynthia asked.

"Well, you see, there's an open space above the board. I got up to look, thinking what a grand place it would be to hide from you. The board came away and I fell down and bumped my head. I've never hidden there because Snorter is always in the way." He stepped on a brace and wriggled over the partition.

Cynthia climbed up and peered down into the dark little cubbyhole.

"I'll hide the flag in the corner," Randy said. "Give me some hay to cover it."

"It'll get all dirty and mildewed," Cynthia objected.

"No it won't. I'll bring out something to put it in."

"I know," Cynthia exclaimed. "Remember that

pretty cherry-wood box that Father made for me, to keep little things in? We'll use that."

"Fine!" Randy laughed. "Sounds as if you were satisfied with my hiding place."

"I think it will be safe here." Cynthia paused a moment before adding, "I'm glad we're not going to burn it. I love it."

"This flag is not for burning; it's for waving," Randy declared. "Some day we'll see it waving free as air."

"You sound so sure," Cynthia said. "You make me feel sure, too. I'd better go back to the house. Can you get out by yourself?"

"Yes." Randy's head popped above the partition. "There are a couple of braces here I can step on. Father must have put them in to make it stronger in case Snorter started kicking."

The bull was looking over the bars into the stall, so Randy had to leave them shut. "We'll take the box in tomorrow anyway. It won't hurt Snorter to stay out tonight."

Mother was silent at supper. Afterwards she seemed to have trouble settling down to work. Several times she went out on the porch. The children had never seen her so restless. "I thought your father would surely be home by now," she said.

Later, she had them recite the twenty-third psalm. Then she got down the prayer book and read a prayer for those in peril.

Randy hoped it would keep his father safe, of course. But Master Bundy was in far greater peril than Father. He hoped with all his heart that Master Bundy would be delivered from peril.

CHAPTER 12

Mother's voice had a lilt when she called them next morning. Father must be home, they thought as they hurried downstairs.

"No, Father isn't home," their mother said. "But Ginger is. Didn't you hear him whinny last night?"

Ginger home without Father? They stared at her in dismay. "Father may be hurt or killed," Cynthia said.

"I don't think so," Mother answered. "I think he left Ginger tied somewhere and he got loose and came home. He's so clever! I'm not worried. I feel much better than I did yesterday. Your father will be home safe and sound; you'll see."

If Mother felt that way, they'd try to. Mother was usually right.

"Of course I thought it was your father come home when Ginger whinnied," Mother said, dishing porridge into pewter bowls. "I rushed out, and I'll admit it gave me a start when I saw Ginger without your father."

"Did you unsaddle him?"

"He's unsaddled, watered and fed. Polly, pet, don't put any more syrup on your porridge. Now let's see, what's to do today? Randy, after the chores are done, you go to the tavern. There might be news. Cynthia, I'm out of rushes, and the pewter only half scoured. You gather some."

"I'll help Cynthia," Polly said.

Her mother shook her head. "You were naughty and climbed the fence yesterday, so you will have to stay in the house today."

Without Polly, this would be a good time to put the flag in the cherry-wood box. When Cynthia went out to get rushes, she carried the little box with her.

"Fine!" Randy exclaimed, when she gave it to him. "I wanted to get that fixed up before Father got home."

They stopped briefly at Ginger's stall to pet him and wonder where their father was.

"You hold the box," Randy said, when they were again in Snorter's stall. "I'll climb down and get the flag." He got on the brace and removed the loose board. With one foot over the partition, he gave a startled yell which was echoed from below.

Cynthia screamed and dropped the box.

"Who—what—" Randy pulled back his leg, but peered bravely into the cubbyhole.

"Randy." It was only a whisper, but he recognized the voice.

"Master Bundy!"

"Don't come down here," whispered the schoolmaster as Randy started to leap into the enclosure.

"Go away and stay away. Forget I am here."

"Does Mother know?"

"Yes. Don't tell her you found me. It would worry her."

Cynthia had been too overcome to speak. Now she asked, "Did you ride Ginger here?"

"Yes. Don't ask any more questions. The less you know the better, in case you are questioned."

"It's not much of a place to stay," Randy said. "You can have the flag to look at. Feel under the hay in the corner."

Master Bundy fumbled under the hay and pulled out the flag. He peered at it in the semi-darkness, then jumped up and held it spread out. "It's beautiful!" His voice was choked. "It's a flag worth fighting for—dying for."

"We think so," Randy said. For a moment they gazed at it in reverent silence. Then Master Bundy said, "Go now, children, and stay away. Leave the flag with me. It will give me courage."

Cynthia handed him the box. "That's to keep it clean and dry," she said.

After he had started to climb down, Randy stuck his head back over and said, "They *were* grand words, weren't they, Master Bundy?"

A chuckle answered him. "Yes, they were grand words, lad. Forgive me for the flogging I had to give you."

"It's forgiven," Randy said. "But you did hit hard."

"You know what I think," he said to Cynthia, when they were outside the barn, "I think Father made that place on purpose to hide in. Oh, I'm glad Master Bundy got there!"

"So am I," Cynthia said. "Of course he'll tell Father about our flag, though."

Randy stopped short. "I didn't think of that!" He stood in thought for a moment. "I'll ask him not to tell when I come back from the tavern."

There were few people at the tavern when Randy arrived. No new bulletins were on the walls. The latest was an account of Master Bundy's flight. He had read it the day before with terror in his heart. Now he reread it in great amusement. It gave a detailed account of how the schoolmaster had been dressed when last seen.

Mistress Estry, busy waiting on trade, told him he'd best not loiter inside. It was no place for boys.

He was at the door when loud talking outside made him pause. "The description's in here. Had it put up myself." That was the squire's voice, and there was the squire coming in the door. And behind him—

"Father!" Randy exclaimed. "Oh, Father, you're safe! Mother sent me to find out."

"Son!" Father's tired face lighted in a smile. He gave Randy a pat on the shoulder and followed the squire to the bulletin board.

"Here it is," the squire said. "Let's see, black broadcloth with velvet collar. White ruffles at neck and sleeves."

"There's no doubt it was Bundy." Father held up a tattered garment with dark stains on it. "There's the velvet collar. One ruffle is gone; here's the other, and the neck ruff." He turned to Randy. "What say, son? Are these the schoolmaster's clothes? You saw him that morning."

"They—they look the same," Randy stammered. "Except his were clean and whole."

A little crowd had gathered. Someone asked, "What's happened? Where's the schoolmaster if those are his clothes?"

"Shot and killed!" the squire announced importantly.

Randy's squeak of surprise went unnoticed in the general excitement.

"Good riddance!" Mrs. Estry exclaimed loudly. "Saves a hanging."

Randy turned toward her, words of hot anger on his lips. He choked them back and turned once more to listen. The squire told the story as if he had been there and done the shooting himself.

Someone cut short his flow of words by asking, "Did you shoot him, friend Stewart?"

Father shook his head. "I knew nothing of his flight until some men I met told me. He would not halt when they ordered, so they had to shoot. They gave me this garment so I could make positive identification. I was quite sure it was Bundy. You don't see many dressed so fine these days."

"Fine feathers don't make fine birds." It was Mrs. Estry again.

"Amen!" agreed the squire. "We were fairly fooled on this fine bird. How came it, friend Stewart, that you could not identify the body?"

"I didn't see it. I met these men some distance from the place where he was shot. I hadn't time to go back. I was on foot, my horse having been stolen. I was anxious to get home lest my wife worry. Their description of the man, and this garment, leave no room for doubt."

"None whatever," the squire agreed. "Good riddance, I say. Now what of the supplies? Did you find the thieves or aught of what we sent?"

Father shook his head. "An almost fruitless mission. No thieves and no supplies. I did, however, find out where the supplies had been stored. It was in a cave at least fifty miles from the route that was supposed to have been used. Right by the river, so I have no doubt that the supplies have gone downstream long since."

"At least we know their hideout," the squire said. "We can keep a watch on it."

"A sound idea! And now, Squire, if you can spare me, I will go home. My journey on shanks' pony was wearisome."

They were well away from the tavern before Randy ventured to speak. "You surely fooled the squire, didn't you, Father?"

Father gave him a sharp look. "How do you mean?"

"About Master Bundy being dead when he is safe in Snorter's stall."

Father asked grimly, "How do you know? Did your mother—"

"No. I—" Suddenly Randy realized the trap he had got himself into. "I showed Cynthia the hidey-hole and there was Master Bundy."

"I see. Yes, the squire is satisfied for the moment. But Bundy must get away as soon as possible. My lack of success in hunting thieves and rebels, Ginger getting home by himself, my bringing in proof of Bundy's death—if the squire's head were not so thick, he'd begin adding these things up and getting an unsatisfactory answer. Well, let us talk of safer things. How goes the work at home now that your school was stopped so abruptly?"

"I've been hoeing weeds when I wasn't hot-footing it between home and the tavern. Mother wanted news of you and Master Bundy."

"It has been a terrible strain on your mother. And there is no sign of its lessening. In fact, we are in greater danger than ever since Bundy was discovered." Father put his hand on Randy's shoulder. "Be extra vigilant in all that you do and say, my boy."

"I will, Father." Randy almost choked on the words as he remembered the flag and Peter Estry's knowledge of it. He came near blurting out the whole affair, but thought better of it. Father had worries enough. So did Mother. So did he, for that matter. How was he going to get a chance to ask Master Bundy to keep still about the flag now that Father was home?

CHAPTER 13

Father quickened his steps as they neared home. Keeping up with his long stride left Randy breathless. Polly, playing in the yard, gave a squeal of delight at the sight of her father.

"Sssh!" he said, lifting her to his shoulder. "Be still as a mouse and we'll surprise Mother."

While their parents were busy talking, Randy beckoned Cynthia outside. "We've got to ask Master Bundy not to tell Father about the flag, before Father can talk to him," he said. "I'll do it right now before I start hoeing. You watch outside the barn. If Father comes, you call as if you were trying to find me."

"All right," Cynthia agreed. "But I'm frightened, Randy. I wish we'd never made the flag. I wish—"

"Hush up and come on," ordered Randy.

Just then his father came to the door. "Good time to get some hoeing done," he said.

With a sigh, Randy picked up the hoe and started for the field. Later, when the supper bell rang, he went to the house, hungry but reluctant. He wished he didn't have to sit under his father's eagle eye. Suppose he had already talked to Master Bundy!

As Randy came by Snorter's paddock, Father stepped out of the bull's stall and closed the bars. Randy braced himself for what might come. All his father said was, "Snorter looks a bit gaunt. I think I'd best grain him for a few days." His smile and wink at Randy said as plainly as words, "You know the real reason I'm shutting him in."

Of course it would make Master Bundy safer from snoopers, but how could Randy get to talk to him? The problem worried him so at supper that he could scarcely eat.

This was so unusual that his mother looked at him anxiously. "You're worn out with the excitement of the last two days," she said. "I want you to go to bed as soon as the chores are done."

Randy didn't mind going to bed after he had made a certain visit. But he needed Cynthia's help. "Can I have some help with the chores?" he asked. "Then I could go to bed earlier."

"Don't look to me for help," his father said, stifling a yawn. "Two nights sleeping on the hard ground make me ready for my own comfortable bed. I'm going to retire as soon as I finish eating."

"I meant Cynthia," Randy said. "She doesn't have anything to do except the dishes. And she didn't have to hoe or run to the tavern."

Cynthia, about to protest, caught his urgent

glance and said, "I'll help you. I can do the dishes later."

"You'll have to be lookout while I talk to Master Bundy," he said as they crossed the yard in the twilight. "Father has shut Snorter in his stall so I can't get in. I'll climb up in the loft and call down. You watch for Father—or Peter Estry. It would be a fine time for him to be snooping around."

He climbed into the loft and leaned down into the hay hole as far as he dared. It wouldn't be a bit of fun to fall on Snorter, who was busy at the manger below him.

He spoke cautiously, "Master Bundy." Then louder, "Master Bundy, can you hear me?"

"Yes, so can your folks in the house, I think."

Randy lowered his voice. "Have you talked to Father?"

"Yes."

"Did—did you tell him about the flag?"

"No." Master Bundy seemed surprised.

"Please don't. I—he—well—"

"Are you trying to say that you don't want him to know about it?"

"Yes. I felt as if I had to have one—"

"Like you felt as if you had to say those words which might have caused serious trouble."

"Oh," blurted Randy, "I'm not fit to live with anyone as brave as Father. I'll burn the flag. I'll be more careful. I'll—"

140

"Don't make promises you won't keep. But try, boy, try as you never did before. As for the flag, I'll dispose of it. Go now, and don't come back. Bear in mind all the time that you hold your father's life in your hands."

"I will. Thanks, Master Bundy. I hope you escape safely."

"Goodbye, and God grant we will meet in happier times, my boy."

Randy came out of the barn looking so unhappy that Cynthia was alarmed.

"What he said hurt worse than any beating he ever gave me," Randy told her.

"Had he told Father about the flag?"

"No, and he will dispose of it. So that worry is off our hands—that is, until Peter Estry tells the squire."

"Randy, don't say such an awful thing. Maybe—"

"Randy, Cynthia," came Polly's voice. "Where are you? I want to help feed the piggies."

Snorter was out in his pen next morning when Randy went to the barn. Ginger was gone.

"Some rebel on his way south must have taken him," Father said.

From his tone, and the twinkle in his eye, Randy knew full well who the "rebel" was.

"I'll take Maje and ride after him," Father went on. "He may have holed up for the night not far away."

It didn't surprise Randy when Father came home at supper time, riding Ginger and leading Maje. "Found him tied to a tree," he explained. "I didn't see anyone. They might have been foraging for food. I didn't tarry to find out."

"The—the rebel couldn't have got far away," Randy said. "He might get captured."

"He might," his father agreed. "There's always a chance. On the other hand he might be rather clever. Yes, he might be hard to catch."

"I hope so," said Randy. "He'll haunt my dreams until I know he got away."

Other events, terrible ones, soon crowded Master Bundy from Randy's dreams. St. Leger with his Indian hordes besieged Fort Stanwix. Even that rabid Tory, Squire Telford, was bitter at the general for using Indians. "They'll take the fort, of course," he said. "And soon as they do, his Indians will pillage the whole Mohawk Valley. Tory scalps will look the same as rebel scalps to those redskins in spite of all St. Leger can do."

Father agreed. "Of course, we are remote from their line of travel," he said. "But we must be prepared in case any come this way. I suggest we strengthen the stockade, lay in a supply of food and ammunition, dig a good well inside the walls, and have patrols on twenty-four hour duty."

"Just what I had in mind," the squire declared. So Beaver Crossing and all outlying farms were

alerted. Meetings were held at which settlers were instructed what to do if danger threatened. Signals were agreed upon. All able-bodied men took turns working on the stockade and putting down a well. The women tended to getting a supply of food, candles and lead bullets stored inside.

Each day terrifying reports came through of Indian raids farther and farther down the Mohawk Valley while the siege of the fort still went on. The Tories were torn between a desire for a British victory and fear of what the Indian horde would do if there was a victory.

Then came the news of the brave advance of the American General Herkimer to relieve Fort Stanwix, the awful ambush into which he fell, and the wounding of the general.

Tories at Beaver Crossing tried to cheer when they heard of his retreat, but it was a feeble effort. Fear of the Indians grew in the little community until it stalked the quiet forest trails like a visible thing. People stayed close to home.

Father gave the family detailed instructions. "I'm likely to be away on patrol duty," he said. "Don't wait for me a minute—not a second. When that church bell peals, start for the stockade. Don't burden yourselves with anything. Don't stop to loose the stock. *Go* as fast as you can. Go all together so there will be no holding back to wait for others." He turned to Mother. "You'll do that, won't you, my dear?"

"Yes, Randall, we'll do just as you say," she promised.

Cynthia and Randy nodded agreement. Polly asked, "Can't I take my dolly? I couldn't leave her for the Indians to get." Tears began to fall at the very thought.

"You may take her if she's where you can lay your hands on her," Father said. "No one must take time to hunt for her."

It was agreed that Cynthia should carry the doll while Randy and Mother took hold of Polly's hands to help her hurry. From that time on, Polly kept her doll on a stool by the door where it could be snatched up instantly.

Father asked Randy to dig a hole in the space behind Snorter's stall. "Your Mother will select the treasures to be put in there," he said. "In case the place is pillaged, they should be safe."

Randy dug a spacious hole and lined it with brick to keep the damp out. He packed the delicate china and beautiful sterling in it along with a few heirlooms. Old blankets were tucked over them and boards laid on top. Then Randy put on a layer of bricks, and lastly dirt and hay.

Days passed, and still Fort Stanwix did not fall. Fear did not abate, however, for the Indian menace remained. It grew worse as the red men became more restless and increased their raids. In the excitement about Fort Stanwix, Burgoyne's advance down the Hudson had been almost forgotten. Now came the news, shocking to the Tories, of the British defeat at Fort Bennington, Vermont.

In the privacy of the barn, Randy did a wild dance of joy. "If only we had our flag now, I'd take it out and wave it," he declared to Cynthia. "Guess the defeat of Ticonderoga didn't end the war like the Tories seemed to think it would. The last chapter hasn't been written yet."

Cynthia shuddered. "No, and it won't be, as long as those Indians are at Fort Stanwix. I can't sleep at night thinking about Indian raids."

"Don't cross bridges until you come to them," Randy said. "They may not take Fort Stanwix."

He was right. A week later, St. Leger's Indians were retreating west, tricked by Benedict Arnold into going home. St. Leger couldn't win without their help so he withdrew, and Fort Stanwix was safe.

To the Tories at Beaver Crossing, his failure didn't seem as important as the withdrawal of the Indians. There was great rejoicing.

The Indian scare was slow to subside. That was why Randy's first impulse was to run when he spied an Indian lurking at the edge of the cornfield early one morning.

CHAPTER 14

There was a thin fog when Randy went out to look at his rabbit trap that morning. It glowed rosy in the East with promise of warmth to come. It was still chilly. Randy shivered as he hurried along. A sudden guttural "Ugh" checked his stride.

Startled, he glimpsed a dark figure behind a tree and whirled to run.

"Boy," came a deep voice, "Grunting Bear brings a message."

Grunting Bear! Randy checked his flight and looked back. It was Grunting Bear all right. There were no other Indians in sight. Relieved, but still wary, Randy turned.

"What are you doing here?" he demanded. "It's dangerous. Everybody is angry at the Indians. If they find you—"

"Grunting Bear know. Bring message to your father. Say to him, 'Acorns are ripe.'"

"'Acorns are ripe'? Sounds silly. Father won't think much of that."

"Father have more sense than son. White Hair send message. Do as White Hair say. Tell father

147

'Acorns are ripe.'" With no further word, the Indian drifted away as silently as a bit of fog.

His words lingered on. "Do as White Hair say." Randy recalled the earnestness of the old man— the burning whisper in the cave, "We must stop the lobsterbacks." He remembered, too, his first meeting with the old man when he had said, "Tell your father acorns will ripen early." That hadn't meant anything to Father. He had thought it some old superstition. *Or had he?* Father might have been pretending.

Randy stood in deep thought while the fog lifted and a red sun peeped over the hill. "Acorns will ripen early," and now, "Acorns are ripe." What did the words mean? What would Father have to do? Would it mean danger for him? If only Father would let him share his work!

Randy stumbled home, still thinking. "No rabbits?" his mother asked, when he came into the kitchen. "I had my mouth all ready for rabbit pie." It was only then that Randy remembered he hadn't looked at the trap.

"I saw Grunting Bear," he said to his father. "He said to tell you that acorns are ripe. The old man sent the message."

"Acorns are ripe." Father flashed his wife a look which Randy could not understand. She seemed startled, but managed a smile and her voice was steady as she repeated, "Acorns are ripe."

It seemed to Randy almost as if she said, "Thy will be done."

Father nodded gravely and went on eating.

"Father," Randy asked, "does the message mean something to you?"

"Yes, son, but I'm not going to explain it to you. Forget that you heard it."

"I haven't forgotten the other one the old man sent you. It was months ago. He said, 'Acorns will ripen early.'"

"Yes."

"You said it was some superstition."

"So I did, so I did. Well, son, you know what I think? It's my firm belief that something awful is going to happen to this ripe crop of acorns." He laughed as he spoke and gave his wife a reassuring smile. "Yes," he repeated, "they ripened too early for their own good.

"This afternoon," he continued, "you shall take a message to the squire for me. Tell him you glimpsed an Indian in the woods and I have gone to hunt him. Of course, you'll not tell him it was Grunting Bear, nor repeat the silly message about the acorns. We wouldn't want to bother the squire with silly superstition, would we?"

"No sir," said Randy, grinning.

Half an hour later, Father had said goodbye and ridden away. It wasn't anything he said which made his departure haunt Randy's memory. It was the lingering way in which he kissed the girls and Mother, and the extra hug he gave Randy. It was the look in his dark eyes, sober, yet exalted and eager. It was Mother's tremulous whisper as he started away, "Ride with him, dear God! Be his shield and buckler!"

His shield and buckler! The words startled Randy. "Father's going to fight, isn't he?" he asked his mother, so low the girls wouldn't hear.

She nodded, her eyes on the rider now almost out of sight. "There—he's looking back," she said. "Everybody wave."

They waved until he had disappeared into the woods. When Randy turned to his mother, a dozen questions hovering on his lips, she shook her head. "What you don't know, you can't reveal in an unguarded moment."

Randy remembered it often in the dreary weeks that followed.

That afternoon, he found Squire Telford in a joyful mood. Word had come that Burgoyne's army had crossed the Hudson.

"Think of it, boy, they're on our side of the river now," he exclaimed. "They'll reach Beaver Crossing before snow flies. Belike I'll entertain the great man right here in my own home."

"Won't the—the rebels try to stop them before they get this far?" Randy asked, hoping he didn't look as sick as he felt.

"Of course they'll try, but what can they hope to do against General Burgoyne and his Regulars? Now what was that word from your father?"

"An Indian?" he protested when Randy had told him. "How could he get past our patrols? Are you sure it was not a figment of your imagination caused by fear?"

Randy, about to deny that he had been fearful, thought better of it. "It was quite foggy and still a little dark—"

"That's it, that's it. No doubt you ran home as soon as you saw this terrible Indian?"

"I whirled right around," Randy admitted. "I didn't even look at my rabbit trap."

"If you had not been in such a panic no doubt you would have seen it was naught but a fog-draped bush. Never let fright get the best of you, lad. When I was your age—"

Randy stood patiently while the squire gave detailed accounts of his own bravery as a boy. He didn't listen. He was inwardly rejoicing that the message had fallen on stony ground. There would be no extra patrols sent out. It would be safer for Father.

He came back to attention in time to hear the squire say, "Ah, well, we can't expect too much of present-day youth. They are too sheltered and protected. Try and control your fears better in the future, lad. See what a wild chase you have sent your father on. I trust he will soon satisfy himself there are no Indians about, and return. Be sure and tell him the good news of Burgoyne's advance."

"I will, sir." Randy got out of the "great man's" presence as quickly as he could. Good news indeed! If only he were a little older so he could get in some good licks against the lobsterbacks! He thrilled to the thought of Father riding Ginger into battle. Master Bundy would be there too. Maybe the old man. He pictured the latter, white-haired and limping as he toted a heavy musket. You couldn't stop such men.

To Squire Telford's surprise, Father didn't get home that day, or the next, or even the next week. He came to the house, grave and kindly, trying not to show the uneasiness he felt. "We're searching everywhere," he told Mother. "Don't you be alarmed, ma'am. Everything's being done that can." He repeated that several times, adding, "If there is aught you need done, let me know and it will be attended to."

Mother thanked him, her handkerchief at her eyes.

He beckoned Randy into the yard and talked to him "man to man." "I didn't want to alarm your mother," he said. "But I am much afraid your father has fallen a victim to the rascally redskins. I can explain his absence in no other way. It must be that you did see an Indian that morning."

Randy held his head down, and spoke as huskily as he could. "Wouldn't there be some sign—something to show? I've looked all around."

"No, lad. They'd hustle him off to their villages in the West."

"If—if Father's alive, he'll get free," Randy quavered. "He's a match for a dozen Indians."

Squire Telford looked at him pityingly and went away.

Randy held his downcast attitude until the squire was out of sight. Then he went into the house, expecting to have a good laugh with his mother over the "Indian scare."

She was in no laughing mood. "His danger is as great as if he were hunting redskins," she declared.

"I wish I hadn't given him Grunting Bear's message," Randy said, depressed by her serious tone.

"No you don't." She lifted her head proudly. "Your father is where he should be, where he wants to be." She seized Randy by the shoulder. "Remember him in your prayers. Pray God for his safety every day." She blew her nose hard, and her voice was brisk once more as she said, "Get back to your apple picking, son. We'll start making cider this afternoon."

Randy looked at her in wonder. Didn't she have any heart? You'd think she'd sit and worry instead of thinking up work for him to do.

September the eighteenth came, and the battle

of Freeman's Farm. It was a decisive victory for the British.

Supper was a sad and silent meal that night. Afterward, Mother searched both Bible and prayer book for comforting passages, finally falling back on the twenty-third psalm.

"There's naught in the whole book more comforting," she said. "Let us say it together loud and clear, not mumbling, but with faith and confidence in every word of it."

The next few weeks were filled with suspense. One thing cheered the patriots, Burgoyne did not continue his advance down the river. The longer he delayed, the better organized would be the opposition against him. Mother, who had been giving Randy and Cynthia daily lessons, stopped them so that Randy could go to the tavern each day for news.

The rest of the day she kept him and herself busy gathering and storing fruits and vegetables for winter use. "Humdrum tasks," she said, "not in tune with our state of mind, but a good outlet for taut nerves."

One day as Randy was looking for late bulletins on the tavern wall, Mrs. Estry approached him. "There's nothing new," she said. "You'd best get out. This is no place for a lad like you."

Randy glared at her, but said nothing.

"Get out," she ordered. "Get out now!"

Randy, so angry he could not speak, turned his back on her and scanned the bulletins once more.

"Lad," came the squire's curt voice from across the room, "Randy Stewart, come over here."

"More instructions!" thought Randy, but he dared not ignore the squire's order. He looked to the far side of the room where the squire was sitting at a table with a British officer. The squire beckoned.

Randy made his way among the tables on leaden feet. At last his sin was going to catch up with him. What should he do? Admit they'd had a flag and destroyed it? Or call Peter Estry a liar? He wished most heartily that he had obeyed Mrs. Estry's order to get out.

The tall, thin man in a British captain's uniform eyed Randy coldly up and down. "I want the truth, boy," he said.

"Captain Rands wants to ask you about your father," the squire explained.

About Father? Randy felt a stab of fear. Then he remembered his mother's words, "What you don't know, you won't tell in an unguarded moment," and felt better.

He looked the captain in the eye and said sadly, "Father is away. He went to hunt Indians. We greatly fear—"

"Where did he say he was going, up river or down?" The captain's steely gaze seemed to be boring into Randy's very brain.

"He didn't say. But the Indians—"

"What did he take with him?"

"His horse and gun."

"No baggage?"

"No sir." Randy was glad he could answer truthfully. He was sure the captain could have detected a lie the size of a pinhead.

"You know nothing more of his intentions?"

Randy felt sweat in the palms of his hands. He kept his voice dull. "No sir. Squire Telford thinks—"

"Never mind what he thinks. Did your father say aught which would make you think he intended to stay long? Did he leave instructions about the crops? The stock? Getting ready for winter?"

"No sir. He said nothing except that he would look for Indians, just as I told the squire that day." He turned toward the squire who nodded gravely.

The captain sat in brooding silence for a time, then moved his head in curt dismissal. "You may go," he said.

Turning to leave, Randy was stopped by his cold voice. "If your father comes home, or you have word of him, notify the squire at once. *At once.* Understand?"

"Yes sir." This time Randy succeeded in getting away. He didn't let himself hurry, much as he wanted to. He even stopped at the bulletin board and took time to read all the old notices. He expected Mrs. Estry to order him away, but she seemed to have lost interest in him.

Homeward bound, he thought over the disquieting interview and decided not to tell his mother. It would worry her and do no good. What had roused the officer's interest in Father? Not fear for his safety. Randy, remembering the cold voice and colder eye of the man, was quite sure of that.

The flag—it must be that, even though he hadn't mentioned it. Probably he wanted to wait and confront Father with Peter's accusation. One thought cheered him. He might have to wait a long time to get after Father. Still, the whole affair made him feel guilty and sick.

He looked so glum when he got home that Mother exclaimed, "Not another defeat?"

He shook his head. "No new bulletins."

"Well, cheer up, son. No news is good news." Then looking at him sharply, she asked, "What happened to put you in such a doleful mood? You look sour enough to curdle milk."

"Mrs. Estry tried to order me from the tavern—but I didn't go."

"Is that all?" laughed his mother. "She had only your good in mind, so forgive her. In truth, the tavern is no place for you, but I must have news."

CHAPTER *15*

"No news is good news," Mother had said. It was "no news" they had to live on the next few days. Randy went each day to the tavern and was thankful not to see the captain or the squire.

Then, one evening as he was coming in from the field, he saw the two of them dismounting from their horses at the yard gate. For one panicky moment, he turned to flee, then straightened his shoulders and walked into the house. He wished, too late, that he had told his mother about the captain. It might make her better prepared for his questioning.

He was in time to hear the squire say, "This is Captain Rands, a loyal subject of the king. He is interested in your husband."

"Oh, Captain, has he been found?" Mother asked. "Has aught been heard?"

"No." The cold voice Randy remembered so well stopped her excited questions. "He has not been found. I have heard something. What it is, I am not prepared to say. Your husband went away when?" He asked many questions. If Mother thought it was strange that most of them were about Father's trip to England, she gave no sign. She answered all questions clearly and courteously and with no hesitation.

"How brave she is!" thought Randy.

At last the captain could think of no more questions and turned to go. "Will you tell me now what you know of my husband?" Mother asked. "Is he a prisoner of the Indians?"

"I can tell you nothing," the captain said coldly, and strode out the door with no word of farewell. Squire Telford lingered long enough to say, "If you see a stranger about the place, don't be alarmed. He is merely watching."

"Watching whom?" Mother demanded. "Us?"

"Not at all, not at all. He will watch that no one molests you. There are many rebels passing on the river."

"I am not afraid. Randy here—"

"He is overly young to protect you. There will be a guard." He followed the captain out of the house leaving the Stewarts looking at each other in uneasy silence.

Mother broke it first. "Guard, indeed! We have no need of a guard."

"He's not here to guard us," Randy burst out. "He's here to catch Father if he returns. They question his loyalty."

"Nonsense!" But there was a hollow ring to his mother's tone.

Randy shook his head. "It isn't nonsense, Mother. And it's my fault they mistrust Father."

"Mine, too," Cynthia said, and burst into tears.

Randy plunged into the story of the flag and its falling into Peter Estry's hands. "I'll go to the squire and explain that Father knew nothing about it," he concluded.

"You'll not say a word," Mother declared. "There's a possibility that Peter hasn't told the squire. Then what a pickle you'd be in by telling. No, we'll say naught about it and forget the rude captain's visit."

From that time on, a guard patrolled the Stewart farm. He did not come near the house, but he could be seen lurking about outside.

"I'd like to turn Snorter loose some night," Randy said.

Though the idea made Mother's dimple pop out, she vetoed it sternly. Neither would she let him roam the woods at night to watch for Father. "You might get caught," she said. "Then we would have some explaining to do."

The days dragged by. Still Burgoyne made no more advance. Randy heard men at the tavern say he was waiting for help from the south. Others predicted gloomily that he would delay so long the rebels would get strong enough to attack him before help could come.

That was what happened. After three weeks'

delay, and no British fleet coming up the Hudson, the second battle of Freeman's Farm was fought. This time the patriots were victorious.

Randy was at the tavern when the news came that Burgoyne was retreating.

"I don't believe it," the squire declared. Later, when the news had been confirmed beyond a doubt, he said, "He'll rally. He's holding off for reinforcements, or belike he'll lead the rebels into a trap. Burgoyne's got a trick or two up his sleeve yet."

Burgoyne's next "trick" was to surrender!

When the squire heard that, he went fairly insane. He declared it was a rebel lie and the man that told it should be shot. Tories fleeing down the river proved beyond a doubt that it was true. Burgoyne's army had laid down its arms and been disbanded. "Better get into Canada before the rebels chase you out," was the warning.

The people of Beaver Crossing, remembering their own treatment of "rebels," decided that was good advice. Even the squire reluctantly agreed.

"Of course we won't be staying long," he said. "The king will send another army and sweep these ragged rebels into the sea. But for now, we had better seek refuge in Canada. Hide your valuables. Take little with you. We will travel fast."

He sent word to Mother to make ready to go. "I'm not going," she told the messenger. "I will stay where my husband can find me."

"Squire says you're going, willing or not," was the answer.

"I'll not go, and you can tell the squire that from me."

Bold words! But that was an anxious night in the Stewart household. "I want you to go to bed early," Mother said. "We'll need all our wits and courage tomorrow."

"Let's hide in the cave in the old quarry until they have gone to Canada," Cynthia begged.

Randy thought that was a good idea. He was as determined as his mother not to go north, but he didn't see how they could hold out against the squire.

"We'll not leave the place to be pillaged and burned," Mother said. "We'll stay here and resist them. God will help us. Maybe—" her eyes shone and her voice had new confidence, "maybe He will send your father to save us. Yes, I think that is the way He will help us. We must pray for it, children, pray earnestly and with faith."

With their mother's confident prayer echoing in their ears, the children went to bed and peaceful sleep. Mother surprised them with griddlecakes next morning, something they hadn't had since Father went away. She had dressed with extra care and was cheerful and smiling. She said grace with simple confidence, "For what we are about to receive, we thank thee, God."

What were they going to receive, Randy wondered uneasily as he went out to milk. Would Father, miraculously brought by Mother's prayers, come hurrying home? Or would Squire Telford and maybe that hateful Captain Rands come marching down the road and drag them off to Canada?

The matter was soon settled. As Randy came out of the milking shed he saw figures emerging from the north woods. He recognized the squire and with him a group of tavern loafers.

He hurried to the kitchen. "Squire's coming," he announced.

"Very well," Mother said. "We are in God's hands." She was so brave it made Randy feel brave. too.

Soon there came a pounding at the door. At a sign from his mother, Randy opened it. The squire strode in.

"What? You are not ready to go?" he demanded.

"I am going nowhere," Mother said.

"Oh yes you are. Boy, go harness your horse and be quick about it. There is no time for fooling."

Randy stood still. "Mother doesn't want to go to Canada."

"She's going whether she wants to or not. She's going as hostage for that traitorous husband of hers."

Now was the time to tell, thought Randy. Now

he must confess about the flag. He swallowed hard and began, "Father—"

"We know all about your father," the squire interrupted. "Get that horse harnessed."

"Please let me tell you. I'm the one. It wasn't Father—"

A roar of laughter from the porch interrupted him. "He's the one," said a coarse voice. "He says so himself. Let's string him up and burn the place."

"Nay, let's look around first," said another. "Might be there are things we could use."

"There'll be no looting or burning," the squire said. "When we come back we want good homes."

"She don't deserve no good home."

"She won't get it. It will be a nice reward for some loyal subject."

"I want my reward now," called someone. "What say, men, why wait?"

The squire raised his voice in protest. The men raised theirs even louder.

In the din, a far-off sound went unheeded by all except Mother. She had been standing calmly by while the men disputed, quite as if it didn't concern her. Now she lifted her head. Her eyes sparkled. "Listen, children," she murmured.

Randy heard it then, swift hoofbeats approaching. Suddenly the others heard it. They fell silent.

"Have your gun ready," the squire said to the

one armed man in the group. "I know not who it is."

Before the man could prime his weapon, a group of horsemen swept around the house. A tall figure in buff and blue uniform leaped off his horse and onto the porch.

Father! And in a captain's uniform! The Stewarts choked back their welcoming cries of joy as Father stepped up to the squire.

"What goes on here?" he demanded. "What is this riffraff doing at my door? Do not draw your gun. My men have theirs ready. What, I say, is going on here?"

Before the squire could collect his wits enough to reply, Mother said, "I knew you would get here, Randall. These men have done no harm—merely been a bit rude. Let them be on their way."

Captain Stewart nodded. "Good riddance. Squire, there are those at the tavern who will gladly speed you and these loafers on your way to Canada."

"To think I nurtured such a snake in my bosom!" spluttered the squire.

Captain Stewart threw back his head and laughed. "Here's another 'snake' you nourished." He pointed to a man in lieutenant's uniform.

The squire's eyes popped. "Master Bundy! Why, you—you're dead."

"Quite observant, aren't you!" The schoolmaster laughed heartily.

"Lieutenant, you stay with me," Captain Stewart said. "The rest of you help these Tories on their way."

After the squire and his followers had been escorted away, Captain Stewart drew his wife and children into his arms. "Looks as if we arrived just in time," he said.

"They had about decided to take what they wanted and burn the house down," Randy told him.

"They were going to take us to Canada," Cynthia added.

Mother looked at him with shining eyes. "I never doubted God would get you here in time to save us," she said.

"And who do you think was God's messenger?" asked Father. "None other than Mrs. Estry. She sent us word of your plight and urged us to come quickly."

"Mrs. Estry?" gasped Randy. "Why, she—she—"

"A stauncher patriot never lived, though Peter did not know it."

Polly, who had been cuddling in her father's arms, pulled at his buff lapels. "Take off these funny clothes and put on your own," she begged.

Her father laughed. "These 'funny' clothes are my own, pet. I expect they will be my work clothes for years to come. Some day, if I work hard enough,

I'll be able to stay home in peace and prosperity, God willing."

"Amen!" echoed Lieutenant Bundy and Mother.

They went into the house and Mother made more griddlecakes. Randy took Ginger and Master Bundy's horse to the barn. "Ginger, I dreamed many times of you carrying a captain in buff and blue," he said, stroking the arched neck. "You should be a proud horse to carry such a fine-looking officer. Father a captain in the American army! Ginger, I'll never be happier than this, even when I get to heaven."

There were so many questions for Father to answer that he didn't have a chance to eat his griddlecakes. "Tell you what, lieutenant," he said, "you eat a stack and I'll answer questions. Then it will be my turn to eat and you carry on." And to Randy, "Fire when ready, son."

Randy wasted no time. "Were you in both battles of Freeman's Farm? Did you see General Burgoyne? Was the old man—"

"Hold up," laughed his father. "You're shooting too fast. Yes, I was in both battles. Yes, I saw Burgoyne. He is now a prisoner of Schuyler in Albany."

"My turn," said Cynthia. "When Washington is made king, will you try and get me made lady-in-waiting to Queen Martha?"

169

"We'll have no more kings in this country," growled her father. "What say you, friend Bundy?"

The latter, his mouth full of cakes, shook his head emphatically.

Randy glared at his sister. "Let's not have any more silly interruptions. Did you know Master Bundy before he came to Beaver Crossing, Father?"

"Yes. We were both on General Washington's staff. We came here for the same purpose and worked together. He arrived a few weeks before I did. No one knew we were acquainted, least of all, you children."

"The old man and Grunting Bear—"

"They were working with us. So was Mrs. Estry —and good service they rendered. The first 'acorn' message meant that the British were gathering more quickly than had been expected. The second told me to come at once to help stop the invasion."

"My turn," Master Bundy said, swallowing the last bite on his plate. "I'll not wait for you to ask questions. Your mother hid me in Snorter's stall, which had been made for such an emergency. You almost gave me heart failure when you climbed in."

"What happened to the old man?" asked Cynthia.

"I got the message he sent through Randy, and had him taken to a safe place to recover from his injuries. He is up at the tavern with Grunting Bear, probably having his first good meal for many a day."

"Were you talking to Father at the barn that night he said Snorter was sick?" asked Randy.

"Yes." Master Bundy laughed. "You gave us a shock that night. We thought it was 'snooping Peter.'"

"That clears up a lot of things," Randy said. "Now I must tell you something, Father. Cynthia and I didn't obey you about the flag. I talked Sis into making one. But we didn't expect to have you considered a traitor because of it."

"What do you mean, son?"

"Peter Estry got hold of the flag. Cynthia had to give him Polly's doll cradle to get it back. He must have told the squire. He and Captain Rands decided you were a traitor. They had the place patrolled day and night to catch you if you came home. That's why they were going to take us to Canada—as hostages for you."

Father shook his head. "It wasn't the flag, though that might easily have caused serious trouble. Some Tories who knew me were at the first battle of Freeman's Farm. They brought word. Mrs. Estry told me."

"I'm glad it wasn't our flag," Randy said.

"It might well have been. It was not wise to have it." Father paused, then added, "However, wisdom is not the only thing which will win this war. There must be fierce devotion, even to the point of recklessness. Don't lose that devotion, son.

171

Before our freedom is won, you will be called on to use it."

"I—I'm ready any time," Randy said, wishing his voice was firm instead of pip-squeaky.

"Where is your flag?" Father asked. "This is the time to bring it out."

"We haven't got it any more," Randy said regretfully. "I realized how foolish I'd been and I thought we'd better not have it in case the squire came looking for it. So I had it disposed of."

He looked at the schoolmaster, who smiled and said, "Yes, I disposed of it. Go look in the southeast corner of Snorter's stall."

"You mean you didn't—"

"I was like you, lad. It was my flag. Sensible or not, I had to cherish it. The southeast—"

Randy was already gone, running at top speed to the barn with Cynthia at his heels.

He had left Snorter in his stall the night before to protect the valuables hidden there. Now he let the bars down, hoping the animal would go into the pen. But the big beast seemed content to lie in his stall and chew his cud.

"What will we do?" exclaimed Cynthia. "We can't go in there. Shall I get Father?"

"No. I'll get in there with a pitchfork."

"Don't you dare, Randy Stewart. If you do, I'll call Father."

"I know what to do." Randy ran to the granary and returned with a bucket of grain. He held it over the fence. "Here, Snorter," he coaxed, "come have some nice oats."

Snorter eyed him drowsily, but made no move.

Randy tipped the bucket so the contents showed. He dribbled grain, all the time inviting Snorter to the feast. Finally, he slammed the bucket down with a bang. "You lazy thing!" he shouted. "I'll have you out of there if I have to use a pitch-fork."

He turned to rush into the barn, but stopped at the sound of laughter from Cynthia. "Look," she said. "I guess you scared him that time."

Snorter didn't look scared, but he was getting to his feet. He switched his tail, then strolled into his pen.

Randy slipped into the barn and fastened the bars. He climbed into the hidey-hole. "Southeast corner," he said. "That's about the only place I didn't dig up when I buried the stuff." He started pawing the hay away.

"Need a stick or something?" Cynthia asked, leaning down interestedly.

"I don't think so. Master Bundy didn't have one. Ooops! Here's something hard. Wait until I get hold of it. Yes, here it is, Sis, here's the little box."

He stood up and opened it. "Here it is, safe and sound." He unfolded the flag and waved it about his head.

"Let me take it while you climb out," Cynthia said. She hugged it close. "I'm never, never going to part with it. I may make others, bigger and even of silk, but I'll never have one I love like this."

Randy said nothing. He couldn't put into words how the little flag made him feel, not without sounding as silly as Sis, and that wasn't for him. He'd soon be big enough to go and fight for his flag. That's the way he'd show what he thought of it.

"Found it, I see," Master Bundy said, when they entered the kitchen.

"Put it where we can all see it," Mother said. "It is a beautiful and inspiring symbol of freedom. Pray God it may wave forever!"

They watched in silence as Randy fastened it above the mantel.

Everyone jumped when Master Bundy brought his hand down on the table with a whack. "Speech time," he declared in his most schoolmasterish voice. "Master Randy, belike you will favor us with a speech today."

"That I will, sir." The twinkle in Randy's eyes matched that in Master Bundy's. His voice was husky as he began, "Is life so dear, or peace so sweet—"

The deep voices of Father and Master Bundy,

174

the gentler voices of his mother and sister, joined him in the solemn pledge, "I care not what others may do, but as for me, give me liberty or give me death."